DUKE AROUND AND FIND OUT

TAMARA

COPYRIGHT

CHAPTER
ONE

London

Arabella Hall excused herself from the after-dinner formalities at the Duke and Duchess of Ruthven's first entertainment and hurried to her room. She quickly changed into another gown. The bodice on her new dress far too low for good company. The mask, and bold rouge on her lips, set the scene for what she needed to accomplish. She glanced in the mirror, nodding at her reflection. She appeared as a woman who was not herself, and should not raise any suspicions if she played the game correctly.

Lady Lupton-Gage would send her packing back to Brighton if she knew what she was about. But what choice did she have? Her brother, a nincompoop with very little common sense, needed her help and had sought her out in town, begging to be saved from certain death.

Not that she thought Lord Leo Wyndham, future Duke of Carnavon, would do as he threatened. He was nobility, a gentleman after all. He could not kill anyone without repercussions.

Arabella used the servant stairs, pleased that they were busy having dinner belowstairs while the family upstairs enjoyed their brandy and cigars and idle conversation in the drawing room. She wished to stay and celebrate Evie's success in town these past weeks, but one night would not hurt.

She needed to steal into Lord Wyndham's library during his scandalous party and burn the vowel of debt before he could use it further against her brother.

It took her only a short time to make the brief journey across Mayfair, the marquess's house glowing with light and bursting with people trying to gain entry. All of whom were disguised in cloaks and masks. Was this entertainment so very risqué?

She had heard from her maid that it was, and yet, surely it could not be so very bad.

Little did Arabella realize how devoid of propriety the party was when she stepped into the foyer. Every room was filled with guests. The laughter, the cloying scent of perfumes that made her eyes water, was almost enough to send her turning about and leaving.

But she could not.

She pushed her way into the ballroom and, from the threshold, could see Lord Wyndham, the only one without a mask, toast his guests, urging the orchestra to play louder, the dancing to be more vibrant, the kissing...

People were kissing? In public?

Arabella schooled her features. Wearing a mask only covered so much of her face, and she was already feeling out of place and the odd one out.

What kind of party was this?

She knew Lord Wyndham to be a scoundrel, a man of loose morals and determined never to settle, but this ball, or whatever it was one called such an event, was like nothing she had ever seen.

It was no wonder her brother was so frightened of the man. He was unhinged.

She walked about the house. At some point, a guest handed her a glass of champagne, and she thanked them, not that she would drink it, but it certainly made her appear as if she were involved with the gaiety.

A closed door caught her eye, and moving toward it, she turned the handle, relieved to find it unlocked. She quickly whipped inside, and as she suspected, the room was the library. The large, mahogany desk and wingback chair behind it told her it was his lordship's private space.

With little time to lose, she raced to the desk and wrenched the many drawers open, searching for the vowel of debt her mindless brother had signed.

Why had he gambled what he did not have? "Stupid, silly clown," she mumbled before wrenching open another drawer with more force than was needed.

"Do be careful with the desk, my dear. It is an antique."

Arabella took in the man who had spoken. Her mouth moved, and yet no words came forth. What would she do?

She glanced toward the window and debated throwing herself through it as he came toward her, shutting each drawer before crossing his arms and staring at her with amusement.

Did he think it comical he had caught her? The man was even more peculiar than she thought.

"Care to enlighten me as to why you're trying to steal from me? I do not take kindly to thieves."

She swallowed, wet her lips, and did the only thing that came into her mind. She ran.

CHAPTER
TWO

L eo wrenched the masked beauty against him. From her perfect nose and luscious full lips, he could see she was hiding a pretty visage under the black mask.

The sweet scent of vanilla teased his senses, and her squirming only accentuated his interest in the chit. "What were you looking for?" He turned her about and met her gaze. Her wide eyes darted about the room, searching for an escape, a way to free herself of this dilemma, but there was none.

He had her in his arms and was not letting her go until he found out what she wanted with his desk and why.

"I was searching for a handkerchief, my lord. You see, my nose, it is running most dreadfully, and I could not find a servant to fetch me one, so I looked myself."

"In my desk... For a handkerchief." Leo let her go and crossed his arms, glaring at her as best he could, considering he'd never heard anything so absurd or amusing in his life. And he had heard many excuses, but this one really was too stupid for words.

"Women do get colds, my lord. Are you calling me a liar?" Her chin lifted in defiance, and he scoffed. The woman honestly could not think he would believe these falsehoods. And that was exactly what they were.

Lies.

"I know everyone at my events, and you were not invited. I gather from your attempt to look the seductress that you're a maid, untouched by men, which is to your credit. However, at these parties, it is not wise to be skulking about, especially when you do not know who may corner you in a dark, empty library."

Her mouth gaped at his words, and she bit her lip. He never wished to frighten any young lady, but when one attended his parties unaccompanied and unused to the goings on that happened under his roof, the chit was clearly missing some of her senses.

She leaned on the desk, quiet momentarily, before her shoulders dropped in acquiescence. "Very well, I did steal into your home and library, but I did so because you left me no choice on the matter."

"I left you no choice? I do not know who you are." But he dearly wished to learn, for anyone who broke into the Wyndham house, which was often termed a house of ill repute, definitely needed a name. "Take off your mask."

"I will not." She clasped the mask with her hands, as if that would stop him from removing it.

He reached for the black silk fabric and ripped it from her head. She stared at him with distaste—not a gaze he was used to seeing from the fairer sex—and it tickled him a little that she was unimpressed with his person.

Most women were impressed with all of him...

"How dare you place your hands on me, my lord. You ought to be ashamed of yourself."

He shrugged and threw the mask on the desk. "And yet, I am not. Explain why you're here before I escort you to the door without that mask to hide your identity and ruin all your chances of a Season." He paused, taking in the young woman. Her gown, as scandalous as she could manage, he assumed, was of the finest-quality silk. A woman from the highest echelons of society and one of his equals. Not that many at his private balls were anything else but the *ton*, it was just that they did not want others to know of their wicked forays.

"You would not dare." She stared at him, steadfast in her belief he'd act the gentleman, and he almost laughed. The fool did not know who or what type of man he was.

He clasped her arm and hauled her toward the door. "Shall we see who recognizes you, and they shall give me your name."

She let out a little squeal of horror and wrenched against him as he dragged her closer to the library door.

"You fiend." And then she did something he never expected. She wrenched free of his hold, jumped onto his back, and started hammering his shoulders. He fell to the ground and the little hellcat, without shame, continued her assault.

Leo turned and attempted to clasp her hands to stop her from hitting him, and eventually, he was swift enough to do so, but not without a claw or two against his face.

"Calm down," he commanded, raising his voice for the first time through their absurd interaction.

"You would ruin me just because I would not give you my name?"

She sat across his pelvis, unaware that with each chastisement that came out of her mouth, her body thrust and teased his groin. Leo ground his teeth, fighting the urge that always overcame a man when a woman as pretty as this one wiggled on his lap.

"Get off," he ordered, letting her go.

She crossed her arms, not moving. Was the woman daft? Did she not know what the position she held did to the opposite sex? He studied her a moment and wondered again how innocent she was.

"Do not try such schemes again, my lord. I will defend myself to the end, and I do not take nicely to bullies, and you, sir, are being a tyrant."

"And you're a thief." He clasped her hips and pushed her off him before standing. She climbed to her feet, and they stared at each other for several heartbeats. Their breathing ragged, their tempers flared.

"I will tell you what you wish to know if you promise to let me go with my mask on. I cannot afford to be ruined. There are people who have sponsored me who would be deeply hurt should I embarrass them."

Leo, for all his wayward ways, was not cruel and unkind. Tough he may be, but nothing else. He would not start to be anything else now. "You have my word. Now explain."

Arabella fought to control her racing heart. The man was a monolith, a Greek god sent to taunt her and show her everything she would never have.

Not that she wanted Lord Wyndham, the future Duke Carnavon from all accounts, but she had hoped to marry a man of similar stature, looks and well, a pleasant manner at least.

She had never seen a more handsome man in all her

weeks here in London, and to be manhandled by one who embodied all her fanciful dreams, aesthetically at least, was indeed unfair.

He had discombobulated her, and she did not appreciate that fact one little bit.

"You have a vowel from my brother, and I was going to steal it. He's an unfortunate soul who gambles away money he does not have. If I took it from you, I thought it would solve at least one problem I'm having this Season."

"Your brother owes me money?" Lord Wyndham strode to the desk, his long legs making short work of the distance. His library was vast. Books lined the walls on dark mahogany ornate shelves. Paintings hung on any other available space, and a portrait of a young man hung over the fireplace. A beautiful room that would look even more stunning in the light of day.

"This one?" He held a note and waved it at her. "From a Mr. Gregory Hall. Is this the one you mean?"

"How many do you have?" At his lordship's less-than-pleased glare, she joined him at the desk. "Yes, that is the one I speak of."

"He owes me five hundred pounds. I will not be forgiving that debt."

It was a lot of money for anyone. She was an heiress, perhaps she ought to pay it and be done with the man, be done with all this absurd business. She could have been ruined this evening. His lordship was right. What if Lord Wyndham had not been the one to find her? What if some other lout had?

A shudder ran through her, and she shook it aside, needing her wits now more than ever to get out of here whole. "I will pay it."

9

"You will?" he asked, surprise in his tone. "You realize that had you accomplished stealing the note, the debt would still stand. I never allow anyone to cheat me, not even a young man whose sister is uncommonly pretty."

"You are not amusing." He laughed at her words, and she ignored that his laugh was more pleasant than expected. "I will have a promissory note from my solicitor to you in the morning. Please ensure you're awake to receive it from my man of business."

"Your solicitor. You have one then?" he said, sarcasm dripping from every word.

"If you must know, I use the same as Lord and Lady Lupton-Gage, whom I'm staying with this Season. A Mr. Tennant will travel here and clear the debt on my behalf."

"How do you know Lupton-Gage?" he asked, his tone no longer one of disdain.

"Lady Lupton-Gage is a distant relative, and I'm Miss Hall."

He barely managed to school his surprise before he blinked and was once again the reputable roué. "You're the heiress from Brighton?"

She sighed, hating that that seemed the only facet of her life anyone seemed to care about. "Yes, the very one. Now pass me my mask, and I shall be on my way. Our association and business are at an end. I wish you well, my lord. Good evening," she said, taking the mask from his hand and slipping it back on her head before striding toward the door.

Away from him and her absurd plan. She should have known it would never have worked. All this sneaking about for nothing. But alas, she would be free of him and her brother's debt by tomorrow, and all would be well.

"Goodnight and pleasant dreams, Miss Hall." The deep

timbre of his voice rattled her more than it had before, and she shivered.

Lord Wyndham could send anyone into a spin, and she doubted she would stop toppling until sleep calmed her mind, and perhaps not even then.

THREE

Arabella thanked the footman, who handed her a missive, and broke the seal. The words jumped out at her: gambling hell, Lord Wyndham, significant loss, brother.

Damn her brother to Hades. Was he born to be a thorn in her side forever? What was wrong with the boy that he would gamble one day after she had settled the debt with Lord Wyndham at no small cost to herself?

Did he think she would always cover his debts? She would no longer be an heiress if she did not stop such support and allow her brother to learn the hard way that some debts had to be paid by oneself.

"A carriage, quickly, if you please." She grabbed her spencer and bonnet and slipped her gloves on as she made her way to the front of the house. Several minutes ticked by before the Lupton-Gage carriage rolled to a stop before her.

Without consideration for her reputation, she ordered the carriage to Lord Wyndham's Mayfair town house and forgot to secure a maid to chaperone. Within minutes, the carriage stopped before the beautiful Georgian home, one of the largest on Berkeley Square.

Arabella frowned, torn as to what she should do. Was her brother still here? Had he lost more? She reached for the missive once again to see who had sent her the warning, but it was not signed.

Had Lord Wyndham even sent it to her?

Doubtful. The man would welcome those who lost their fortunes at his hand. He certainly seemed determined always to make one pay their debts, her brother no different.

Arabella opened the carriage door and jumped down onto the sidewalk. The house loomed high and imposing, much like its owner, and, rallying her nerves, she walked up several steps and knocked.

A butler in blue livery opened and stared down his long nose at her with distaste. "Lord Wyndham, if he is home. Tell him Miss Arabella Hall from the Lupton-Gage household is here to see him."

At the mention of the marquess, the butler's stern visage eased, and he stepped aside, allowing her to enter.

The sound of male voices, mixed with feminine giggles reached her, and she swallowed, feeling out of place and unwanted.

The butler walked toward a back parlor before the chatter was silenced. No doubt, the mention of her arrival had caused much interest before determined, heavy strides sounded on the tiled floor.

Lord Wyndham himself came about the corner. His brows rose, as if he had not believed his butler was telling the truth of her calling.

"Lord Wyndham." Arabella dipped into a curtsy, remembering at least that was proper etiquette. Not that her being here was. "I received a note my brother is here, losing, and I've come to fetch him before I owe you even more of my inheritance."

His lips twitched before he sauntered toward her, reminding her of a wild animal searching for its prey. "Your brother has already lost one hundred pounds this day, and the games have only just commenced. I suggested to him that he leave and no longer gamble on his sister's goodwill, but he does not seem inclined to do so, and what am I to do about it? He is not my problem to bear."

Arabella sighed. There was no use for her sibling. He would forever have this trouble, and nothing she could do or say would change that. "Please go and fetch him. I wish to speak to my brother, if you will."

Before the marquess could do as she asked, her brother joined them, his cheeks blooming a rosy hue that told her he understood his lousy form.

"What are you doing here, Bella? This is no place for you to be unchaperoned."

"And this is no place for you to gamble with funds you do not have," she countered. "I will not pay for your debt again. Do you understand? Should you stay and lose more money you do not have, I will cut you off from any financial support."

"You would not be so cruel." Her brother looked to Lord Wyndham, as if he would support his claim, and yet the marquess merely looked at her brother with disinterest. "You remember what it was like to be poor, sister. Now, I have a chance to earn my fortune. Our distant uncle left me nothing and you everything. It is only right you give me the chance to earn my future."

"You will not have a future this way. You are not a sound

card or dice player. We have not had the ability to learn to play well with our upbringing. You must see sense."

"Your upbringing?" the marquess questioned.

"We were in servitude before inheriting my small fortune, my lord. If you mingled with the *beau monde* instead of the *demimonde*, you would know this already."

"You were in service?" He paused. "Do you mean to say you were a housemaid?"

Arabella raised her brow at his lordship, disliking the stupefaction in his tone. "I was a housemaid, my lord, in a gentleman's home in Brighton. And Frederick, a footman if you must know," she said, turning to her brother. "Fred, I have explained before, but I see I must do so again. The reason our distant relative did not leave you any money was because he did not know you existed."

"A poor excuse if I do say so myself," her brother sulked.

Arabella sighed. "You must return home with me, and we will look at ways in which you can start earning your fortune. There are many ways for a young man like yourself to do well. You do not need to gamble to be like the lords and ladies who surround us so much now."

"Easy for you to say since you already have your fortune." Her brother turned on his heel and started back toward the back parlor where, no doubt, the day's card games were taking place. "I shall gamble or be damned. You do not need to support me anymore, my dear. I shall be perfectly fine."

"Frederick," she called, but her brother was gone and no longer listening to her. "How could you allow him to join in on the games when you know he has no money of his own?"

"It is not my duty to say yes or no to a gentleman who wishes to play. I am not your brother's master."

"No, but you know that he does not have funds. That it is my money that he relies on. I will not pay again. I hope you know that."

"And if you do not, then your brother will have to. Of course, I'm more lenient than others, so I warn you now, Miss Hall, that should your sibling continue to lose, you may find young Frederick has no future at all."

"Are you warning me that something terrible will befall my brother?" Arabella clasped her stomach, hating the thought of such evil. Her brother was a nincompoop, but he did not deserve to be beaten or killed merely because he could not pay his debts as quickly as others might like.

"I warn you to ensure your brother chooses wisely whom he gambles with, that is all. London is not all pretty tree-lined streets as you find in Mayfair. There is a seedier side, a dark, dangerous side not for the faint of heart or those unable to pay their debts."

Arabella bit her lip, her stomach in knots at the thought. What if she could not stop her sibling's wayward ways? Whatever would she do? She could not lose him. She went up to Lord Wyndham and clasped his arm. "Please, I beg you, my lord. Help me stop Frederick from gambling. I was hoping you would not allow him to join your games, send him on his way. Tell all you know to exclude him as well. I shall ask Lord Lupton-Gage to secure him employment, and in time, I hope this folly will burn out of his blood."

Lord Wyndham looked down where her hand clasped his arm, and she let go, hoping she did not offend him. He crossed his arms and studied her, thought of her request for several heartbeats.

"And what shall I get out of this arrangement if I'm to

do as you ask? I'm not the type of gentleman who does anything without compensation."

"You want more money?" she asked, aghast at the thought it was what he'd want. Was every male in London so obsessed with wealth?

He chuckled. "No, not money. But I would settle for a taste of your pretty lips. Just once. I admire beauty, and you possess quite a lot of it."

"You want me to kiss you in payment for helping me?" Arabella's heart stopped beating, and heat bloomed over her body. She could not kiss his lordship.

He was far too handsome.

Far above her reach, even for an impromptu kiss.

"I do. Here and now."

She swallowed, rallied her nerve, and leaned up to do as he pleased. There was no one about, no one to see, and it was a small favor that would be over in a moment.

Just before their lips touched, he set her back, shaking his head. "I did not say I wanted you to kiss my lips..."

H e was being a cad, and rightfully so. He deserved the stinging slap that landed across his face a moment after he uttered the words. Of course, he knew a little prim-and-proper miss would never kiss him where he really wanted her to, but it was always worth a try.

"I'm leaving. You, sir, are a disgraceful human being, and I do not want your kind of help."

He watched her storm out of his house, slamming his front door with enough force that the chandelier rattled above him in the foyer. Leo returned to the gambling but did not take part. Instead, he watched Miss Hall's brother gamble away the money he did not have. The young Frederick Hall certainly seemed to believe his sister's money would save him at every turn.

Perhaps he ought to help her. Do one honorable thing in his life. His father would hate that he helped anyone and was kind to another living being, which made the temptation all the more alluring.

He liked nothing more than to irritate his father now that he could no longer touch him.

He inwardly chuckled at his musings.

After several minutes, he grew bored with the games and left to secure himself away in his library. His butler had laid out his many invitations for this evening and the weeks ahead. Poor Thomas, always trying to right Leo's ways, get him to partake in good society, not the naughty kind he was used to, and gain a wife and children.

It was not in his future, not if he could help it. If only to nettle his father even more by not giving him what he, too, wanted—an heir who would carry on the Carnavon name. Not that he would ever let the duke come within a hair-breadth of his children.

If it were the only way he could strike out at his sire, he would make the ducal line die with him. His father deserved nothing less.

An invitation to the Connors ball, the silver-embossed lettering flickered in the daylight, and he lifted the heavy parchment to read it. The ball was to be held this very evening.

Leo tapped the invitation against the desk and stared out the window. Would he go? Give the *ton* something else to talk about. No doubt he would undoubtedly see Miss Hall again if he did.

And apologize to her...

Yes, he supposed he did need to apologize for his behavior toward an innocent woman. But she was amusing at least and determined, not the usual kind of lady who graced the floorboards of London this time of year.

Her humble beginnings mayhap gave her a little back-bone and spice. Not that Leo thought there was anything wrong with being a strong, independent young lady in society. If anything, he respected her attempt to save her brother and her fortune at the same time.

Decided, he slipped the invitation into his pocket and would notify his valet of his decision to attend. No doubt his servant would welcome the change in routine in getting him ready for a society ball instead of one of his scandalous routs.

A rabella stood beside Reign and fought off the despair that another evening would pass, and she would not have danced with enough gentlemen to fill half her dance card.

Worse was the fact she knew the reason why. In fact, there were probably two reasons why she had become a pariah of society, and not one to consider for a future bride.

Her brother and his disgraceful gambling acts and debts that were popping up all over London like the plague had all those hundreds of years before. The man was a menace, and she would have to deal with him sooner rather than later, before there was no money left for her to help him.

The second was her humble beginnings. Even though Evie had managed to marry well, she was far prettier than Arabella and had met one of the last wonderful, eligible men in England.

The pickings were slim in this society. Many gentlemen she thought appeared interesting enough to converse with had long ago married and left for their country estates.

What was left in London was far from promising, and she refused to marry just anyone. She wanted a love match, to be adored just as Reign and Evie were in their unions.

Nothing else would do.

Murmurings and gasps rolled throughout the ballroom

like a wave, and Arabella glanced toward the door to see what was causing the commotion.

Heat kissed her cheeks, her breath hitched, and Reign glanced at her when the sound she thought she had made in her head popped out of her mouth.

"Are you well, dearest?" Reign asked, reaching out a comforting hand.

"Perfectly fine. Just surprised like everyone else that Lord Wyndham is here."

"He is?" Reign's gaze whipped toward the door, her eyes wide with surprise. "Well, he has not attended a ball for some years. Maybe he's decided it's time to find a wife and marry. He will be the future Duke Carnavon, after all. Heirs must be begotten."

"I doubt he's here to find a wife. More likely, the man is here because he enjoys his notoriety." The fiend. Even now, hours after she had left his house, she was still irritated by his request.

Kiss him, indeed.

She still could not think of a location where he thought she ought to kiss him instead. The cheek? His neck? Where else was there to kiss a man?

She frowned and was startled out of her musings when the fiend himself stood before her, bowing.

"Lord and Lady Lupton-Gage, a pleasure as always." He turned his attention to her and smiled warmly, yet his eyes burned with mischief and amusement. "And may you introduce me to your friend. I do not believe we've met."

"Of course, Wyndham," Lord Lupton-Gage said, gesturing to Arabella. "This is my wife's cousin, Miss Arabella Hall, from Brighton. Arabella, this is Lord Wyndham."

She dipped into a curtsy and tried to look interested in

the introduction, but could not. The thought that he may let it be known she had called on him, asked for help, snuck into his library, and tried to steal from him, left her at sixes and sevens. Her heart thumped wildly, and she fought not to have an apoplexy on the spot.

"A pleasure," she managed to mete out.

"The pleasure is all mine," he returned, the cocky grin back on his handsome face.

Arabella wanted to stomp her foot. Did he need to be as handsome as he was? Dark, wavy hair dropped over one eye as if he'd spent hours teaching it to do so merely to make ladies' hearts flutter. His chiseled jaw, full lips, and straight nose. The man was an Adonis, and life was unfair when one was born with privilege and also looks.

"I wonder if Miss Hall would care to dance? The next is to be a waltz."

Arabella shut her mouth with a snap and looked to Reign, who seemed so pleased that her smile was vast, the likes of which Arabella had never seen. "Miss Hall would be delighted," Reign said, placing Arabella's hand on Lord Wyndham's when she did not move.

With little choice, she allowed him to guide her onto the dance floor. His arms engulfed her, pulling her against him in what felt far too intimate and close for her senses to remain aloof and alert.

He was too large, too tall, and imposing. Gosh, he was just too *everything*. She took a fortifying breath and met his gaze, his studying hers with an intenseness that left her reeling.

What was he thinking?

"At the very least, you ought to appear to enjoy our dance, my dear. I am a future duke, after all. One would think a lady such as yourself would be pleased indeed."

"If I did not know what kind of cad you were, perhaps I would be pleased. However, I know your true character and find you lacking."

"Harsh words indeed. I shall have to change your mind about me."

Arabella scoffed. "Unlikely, my lord. But you're more than welcome to try."

FIVE

L ater that evening, Leo watched as Miss Hall remained a wallflower, forever waiting for a gentleman to notice her despondence and ask her to dance.

His heart panged a little at her lack of suitors. Why was no one asking her to dance? She was a beautiful woman, her long, brown locks tied up in a motif of curls with diamond pins that glittered under the candlelight. She had a sweet nose, and large eyes that he could see were losing hope each time a gentleman passed her by. She had an ample dowry; he had made inquiries at his club before coming here. Her lack of suitors did not make sense...

He wandered through the room, partaking in a glass of champagne when it was offered by a footman, and listened to the conversations that flowed about him. Most of them were irrelevant and nonsensical, but one caught his attention and could be why Miss Hall was an unfavorable match.

Her brother.

The debts he was raking up over London that even he did not know about, nevertheless his sister. The lad would ruin her, and most gentlemen agreed with that surmise and would not bet on there being any dowry left by the time they walked her down the aisle.

He stopped by a group of young bucks, who welcomed him. They were more than happy to include Leo Wyndham in their group, hoping he would invite them to one of his parties.

Perhaps he would, depending on what he could learn from them first.

"Good evening, gentlemen. What is new with you all?" he asked cheerfully, knowing they were only moments ago speaking of Miss Hall.

"All is very well, Lord Wyndham," Lord Freemont stated, smiling. "We were just telling of Mr. Frederick Hall and how he owes young Spencer here quite a sum."

"Really?" Leo feigned curiosity and surprise, but it did not astonish him. Miss Hall's brother was moving into dangerous waters he doubted the fool knew how to navigate.

"Yes, unfortunately," Lord Spencer said, confirming his friend's disclosure. "I will not disclose the amount, but it is more than I'm willing to let pass. But I dare not breach the debt with Lord Lupton-Gage, for I do not know if he knows Miss Hall's brother and his gambling habits."

Leo did not think Lord and Lady Lupton-Gage knew anything was amiss, yet they should, if only to help Miss Hall.

"A shame for Miss Hall," Freemont interjected. "Should she be penniless by the time she accepts a marriage proposal, I doubt there is a gentleman in London who would marry her knowing her humble beginnings."

"She was a housemaid, I heard. What a turn of fortune

for one so young," another young gentleman said, whom Leo did not recognize.

"Not that it will make much of a difference to her should she keep bailing out her brother. There will be nothing left," Freemont concluded.

"So none of you would marry her should she be penniless merely because she was a housemaid?"

"Would you?" Lord Spencer scoffed. Leo glared and was glad to see the young man's cheeks bloom the same color as the rose.

"I do not know her well enough to offer my hand, and I'm not looking for a wife. But that does not mean I would discredit her so strongly just because she came from no connections or money." At least he hoped he would not.

"The future Duke Carnavon would not marry a housemaid. I would wager my fortune on that," Freemont declared.

"Do not gamble with funds you cannot afford to lose," Leo warned, glad the young man stopped his lips from uttering anything else foolish.

"Very well, I heed the warning, but she was a housemaid," he whispered after a time. "No amount of money will change that humble past. And although her cousins married well, it does not change who they once were. Granted, Lady Lupton-Gage had a better upbringing than Miss Arabella and Miss Evie Hall, but should she lose the only link she has to this society through her brother's foolishness, she will have nothing. No man from a good family, titled or not, will consider her."

As much as Leo wanted to argue the point, he could not. They were right, of course. The lady required help to stop her brother from gambling, which could enable her a promising, secure future and make her more desirable to those in this society.

You could always show interest, and then others may follow.

She would be married before the end of the Season, and he would ensure her brother was sent away to work before he could gamble any more of what he did not have.

"If you will excuse me, gentlemen, I wish you a pleasant evening."

They mumbled their goodbyes, and Leo went in search of Miss Hall, who was no longer standing with Lord and Lady Lupton-Gage. He glanced over the sea of heads, grateful for his height, and spied her slipping out onto the terrace through the open doors at one end of the ballroom.

He followed her, needing to discuss her troubles she may or may not be aware of. Even so, he could help her, and she could, in turn, help him. An arrangement that would suit them both.

A rabella stepped out onto the terrace and started toward the gardens. Lanterns lined the gravel path, and she strolled along it, passing couples as they returned indoors.

Few took heed of her, an outcome that had become far too familiar to her these past weeks. Last year's Season had been more fulfilling and hopeful. This one was dreary, and she could not help but feel something was wrong that the gentlemen did not like her anymore, or did not wish to court her at all.

But why?

That she could not reconcile.

"Miss Hall?" Lord Wyndham's deep, familiar baritone

pulled her out of her despondent mood, and her heart jumped at the sound of his voice.

"Lord Wyndham, what are you doing out here?" she asked, looking about to see if anyone noticed her alone with him.

He took her arm, and they continued farther into the gardens, but remained within sight of the terrace for respectability. He greeted a couple walking past, and they smiled, their eyes widening, noting it was Arabella he was escorting and not some duchess worthy of his hand.

"I came to see you." His lips pursed, and a slight frown settled between his brows. Even contemplating the troublesome thought that he was, he was still one of the most handsome men she had ever beheld.

She took a calming breath, needing to keep her wits about her, especially with Lord Wyndham at her side.

"I have made some observations this evening that I find worrying." He paused, pulling her to a stop. "Are you always ignored at balls and parties? I have not seen you dance, save for the one we shared."

Heat kissed her cheeks that he had noticed such an embarrassing reality, and she wished herself anywhere but before him and under his scrutiny. "I am not of their class, my lord. No amount of money will make me so, either. It comes from breeding, connections, and good marriage. I have none of those, as you well know."

"But you have a fortune."

"I do, but it does not appear any gentleman wishes to gain it through marriage this year. I do not know the reason why."

"I can tell you why if you do not mind me speaking frankly."

"Of course, please do." What he was about to say could

injure her, but she needed to know if she could right whatever wrong had befallen her. She could not rely on Lord and Lady Lupton-Gage to sponsor her another Season. That would be unfair indeed.

"I think it is your brother that is causing you strife. Men would marry you, humble beginnings or not, but with the threat of your brother spending your dowry before marriage or dealing with his misgivings afterward, I do not think they want the trouble."

His lordship's words were as she feared, but what could she do? There was little she could do to change her circumstances or her brother, who seemed determined not to listen.

"What do you suggest then?" she asked, at a loss.

"I have a proposition. But it would help if you had an open mind to hear it. Do you have one of those, Miss Hall?"

"Of course," she said without delay. "Let me hear of this proposition, and I shall give you my reply."

"Very well then, now, what I suggest is this..."

CHAPTER
SIX

Lord Wyndham led her back toward the house at a sedate pace that gave them time to discuss this plan he thought so highly of, if his inspired expression was anything to go by.

"Well, since you ask, Miss Hall, let me enlighten you on how we can serve each other. You wish to marry for love, I assume."

"That is correct, my lord. Does not everyone wish for such a happy life?" She could not imagine marrying a man who did not love her, who only tolerated her humble beginnings, and only saw her for what wealth she would bring to the union. Such a marriage would not be happy, leading to unpleasantness and despair.

"Whereas I do not wish to marry at all. I find my lifestyle to be one of gaiety and pleasure, two things I doubt I shall find with the gaggle of debutantes who grace the boards within the house before us." His gaze slipped over her like a caress, and his lips twitched into a smirk. "Of course, I exclude you from those I just described. You have already proven yourself to be singular and different, which is to your credit, but even so, that does not mean I wish to marry you either."

Arabella waved his words aside, losing a little patience with the man. "Do tell me this objective, my lord, before I'm too old to marry anyone."

He chuckled. "Touché, Miss Hall. Very well, now, where was I... Oh yes, I do not wish to marry anyone, but if I court you, that will make you far and above desirable to the fools who currently avoid you. Men will want you because I desire you. Simple and foolish, but no one said these bucks currently indoors had any intelligence."

"You're going to pretend to court me to make me more desirable among our set?"

"Exactly what I propose. Being back within society's bosom will also give me respectability. This may surprise you, Miss Hall, but I do not like people being mistreated, as I feel you are being. Life is to be enjoyed, not feared, or to bring pain and sadness. I want to see you enjoy your Season before you marry."

Arabella pulled him to a stop. She glanced up at him and tried to fathom whether he was serious. "But what is in it for you? You do not owe me anything. I'm in your debt after you agree to help me with my brother."

He shrugged, nonplussed. "Well, what fun we shall have, causing a little gossip within the *ton*. It will keep the marriage-minded debutantes from my side at balls and parties, one of the reasons I do not attend such events, and will enable me a little respite from anyone wishing to make a match. And I like you. I think we are friends, are we not? Sometimes, a gentleman does not need a slew of reasons to be kind."

Arabella scoffed, unable to believe that was true of most people, especially in the society she now circulated within.

But, he did make a good point, and it would help her marry sooner and possibly to a gentleman who loved her if she got to know him better. Something she had been unable to do so far this Season with all the distractions of her brother.

"Very well, I shall agree to this venture. To the *ton*, you shall appear smitten, courting me before making me an offer of marriage, and we shall see if any gentlemen take it upon themselves to be your competitor."

"And I shall be left alone, which is what I like most of all, and I'll also be able to keep abreast of what your brother is up to. The young bucks who enjoy gambling their father's money away will alert me of anything you are unaware of. With luck, before you send him away to the country, we can halt his gambling and keep your dowry safe."

Arabella sighed, wishing life could be as easy as Lord Wyndham made it sound, but she could not help but feel doubtful about her brother. Already, whispers this evening had reached her that he had gambled more funds away than he could pay.

"I will speak to Lord Lupton-Gage tomorrow about sending him to the country, where he may be less inclined to gamble. But I do not hold much hope in saving him from his vice. He does not listen to me."

"We shall make him listen," Leo stated, not wanting to let Miss Hall down for reasons he did not entirely understand himself. He supposed his childhood, being ostracized by his father, constantly on the edge of being reprimanded for merely making too much noise while chewing food, could make one feel for the underdog.

Perhaps it was her humble beginnings that her fortune had turned for the better, only to be threatened by an idiotic brother from whom he wanted to save her. Or perhaps for his selfish means of helping her to spite his father, who would hate that he was being so kind to a woman he would not see as worthy of becoming a duchess.

"Shall we return to the ball and dance? If we dance a second time this evening, it will ensure the gossip commences about my interest. It's better to start now than later. The sooner we have you married, the better for everyone."

"I would enjoy that very much, thank you, my lord."

He escorted her indoors, and several guests glanced their way, their eyes widening in surprise that he was still at the ball and dancing with a lady, not once but twice.

He smiled down at Miss Hall, pretending to drink in her handsome visage, which he could not deny was, in truth, very attractive. She was one of the prettiest women he'd ever met. He had also enjoyed ogling her figure when coming across her in his library, bent over his desk, rummaging through his drawers.

He had almost come up behind her, pressed against her perfect ass, before common sense had come over him, and he had questioned her instead.

No, courting Miss Hall would be no chore, and he would enjoy his time back in society at her side. He pulled her into a minuet, and they danced and weaved through other couples on the floor.

Each time they came together, he ensured his hand lingered on hers, or on her delicate waist, his gaze slipping over her like a caress.

She did have a delicious, ample bosom that jiggled a little with each hop or step they took.

Stop being such a cad. You do not want to insult her.

True, but he was a rogue, a man used to ending an

evening of flirtatiousness with a night of debauchery, rigorous sex, and many, many releases, and not just his own.

"You are very beautiful, Miss Hall. Has anyone ever told you such a truth?" he asked, his voice deeper than he had meant it to be. Damn, he wasn't actually interested in her in truth. He would need to remind his body of such a fact.

"No," she answered, her cheeks dimpling in a smile. Her eyes flicked to his, and he saw she was telling the truth. "You are the first, even if you are merely acting."

"Oh no, I'm not acting when I say such things. You are beautiful, and should I be looking for a wife, you would have been one to consider, as I would hope I would be the type of gentleman who may catch your eye."

"You?" She chuckled. "You would catch even a deceased lady's eye, my lord."

"Oh dear, I do not think that is a requirement, but I appreciate the compliment, as macabre as it is."

"You're very welcome," she said without remorse, making him like her even more.

CHAPTER
SEVEN

Arabella sat before Lord Lupton-Gage and Reign and prayed they would help her with her brother's vice. "So you see, I cannot control him, and he will not listen to reason. Why, just this morning, I received a missive from Lord Craig stating that Frederick told him to request funds from me, that I was good for them. I'm at a loss as to what to do."

"Oh, my dear, this is dreadful." Reign came over and took her hand, holding it in support. But she would need more than words and hand-holding to repair the damage her brother inflicted on her finances.

"We could send him to our country estate, and I could have my steward teach him financial accountability there. But would he go? That is the question. He is not a boy, but a grown man."

"I know, and I have broached my concern with him, but I do not think he is receptive to listen."

"No, my dear. I shall speak to Frederick and warn him that should he continue being reckless as he is, all financial support will be removed, and he will end his days in debtors' prison and not a gambling den he's so fond of."

Arabella cringed at the thought of her brother imprisoned, but maybe that is what it would take for him to see sense.

Nothing else she had done had helped.

"Thank you, my lord. You have no idea how much more at ease I am hearing you will try to speak to Frederick. I think because we were always so poor and there were never any funds for such luxuries as gambling, for him, in any case, this life is all new and exciting. It has gone to his head a little, and he has lost his way."

"I can hear your love for your sibling, Arabella, and I will do all I can to help you. I shall report on how I go when I speak to him next."

"Thank you." Arabella excused herself, and seeing the day was cloudless and warm, she grabbed a bonnet, spencer, and maid, and decided to go to the park across the road.

She would walk the graveled paths for a time and try to remove the cloying fear that her brother would not listen to reason and ruin himself before the Season's end.

Within minutes, she was in the park and walking the paths, allowing the dappled light to warm her skin and soothe her worries. All would be well. With Lord Lupton-Gage helping her with her brother and the marquess and his mad scheme in getting her married, the Season would work out, and she would not have to rely on Lord Lupton-Gage and Reign and their generous heart a third year.

The idea of being sponsored yet again sent a chill of revulsion down her spine.

"Miss Hall, I was just coming to see you," Lord Spencer stated, pulling her from her musings.

"Good afternoon, Lord Spencer. I did not know I was to entertain you this afternoon. I hope I have not forgotten an appointment."

"No, I apologize. I should have mentioned I do not come to see you for a joyous reason. Unfortunately, I have come because of your brother. We gambled, you see, in Whites. He gained an invitation through Lord Mellows and joined in on the fun. In any event, he said you were good for the money he lost."

Arabella stood, stupefied, unable to believe Lord Spencer would ask her for her brother's losses in a public park. She supposed he would call, but could he not have waited?

She glanced about and thankfully did not see anyone taking an overly interested view of their conversation. "How much did he lose, my lord?" She was scared to even venture to ask.

"Two hundred and twenty pounds, Miss Hall. Can you please have the funds sent to this address?" he said, handing her his card. "By tomorrow, if you will."

Arabella bit her lip, staring at the card and fighting the tears that welled and made her vision blur. Thankfully, Lord Spencer turned on his heel and left, leaving her to compose herself alone.

She swiped at her eyes when she was sure no one was looking, but it did little to help soothe her. Her brother would ruin them both.

"Miss Hall?" Dread made her stomach clench that another gentleman was going to accost her in the park and demand more monies.

Dear Lord in heaven, please do not be the case.

"Did I hear correctly that Lord Spencer just asked you to pay off another of your brother's debts?"

Arabella sighed in relief at seeing it was only Lord Wyndham, and no one else. "Yes, I'm afraid that is so."

Before she could say another word, he started toward Lord Spencer, who was almost at the park gate, yelling for him to halt and wait.

Arabella followed, unsure what Lord Wyndham was going to do.

Please do not make a scene. Please do not cause unrest in this peaceful park...

"Lord Spencer," Lord Wyndham stated when they had finally caught up to the young man. His lordship turned, a small, pleased smile on his lips that Lord Wyndham had chosen to speak to him, and yet, from the dark, annoyed visage of the marquess, Arabella couldn't help but guess that Lord Wyndham was not going to partake in a pleasant conversation.

"Please explain to me as a fellow gentleman when it became appropriate to accost young, unmarried ladies in the park with requests for payment by people of age and quite capable of paying their debts?"

Arabella gaped. Heat kissed her cheeks, and she looked around, hoping no one had heard the marquess's stern, chastising words.

She did not want everyone to know that Frederick could not control his gambling and that people were asking her to pay for the debts.

How mortifying.

"Lord Wyndham, I thank you for your concern, but it is not your burden to bear," she tried to explain.

"It is not yours either," he snapped, not moving his scowl from Lord Spencer.

"I, ah, I apologize, Miss Hall. I merely thought—"

"You did not think at all; admit it, man. You owe

38

Miss Hall more than an apology, and if you think she will be paying any more debts that her brother racks up, you may think again. Tell your friends that Mr. Hall is responsible for the troubles he draws to himself, and Miss Hall will no longer be funding him out of them."

"Of course, my lord. Again, my sincerest apologies, Miss Hall," Lord Spencer fumbled, backing away from the marquess as if he could not get away from them quickly enough.

Arabella was glad when they were alone once more. The fewer people who saw the interaction or heard what was being said, the better.

"Just as Lord Spencer has done wrong, so have you, Lord Wyndham. You cannot chastise gentlemen so in public. Certainly not on my account."

"But I can, of course. We're courting, are we not? I would defend you should that be true, and if we want the *ton* to believe us, this was a perfect opportunity for the *ton* to see I'm in earnest."

Arabella nodded, hating that he was doing it only out of obligation and because of their plan to get her married and nothing else. How nice it must be for women to have a man love them and want to defend them without any obligation other than that of their heart.

She supposed she could only hope to find such a man with the marquess's help.

"Very well, thank you, and with your warning to Lord Spencer, mayhap he will return to White's or Brooks's and tell everyone he knows that Frederick does not have the means to pay his debts. If he does not change his ways, we will merely stop him from taking part in them to begin with."

"A perfect plan indeed, now," Lord Wyndham said, holding out his arm.

Arabella entwined her arm with his before they again started along the path.

"A turn about the park for all of the matrons of the *ton* to see, and then I shall walk you home. That should satisfy their gossiping tongues for the day."

"Sounds most pleasant," she said, wishing that, in truth, their stroll was heartfelt and wanted. Not merely a means to an end.

CHAPTER

EIGHT

As much as he wished it otherwise, the moment he stepped into the Jenkins' ball later that evening, Leo was disappointed to see Miss Hall yet again standing beside the wall, alone and without even a female friend nearby willing to talk to her.

She was an heiress, a beautiful one at that. Did it matter so much that she had humble beginnings? He frowned, wishing several people good evening before making his way through the throng of guests.

Hundreds of people were present, many of whom he knew from his wild entertainments. He spoke to very few as he headed toward Miss Hall, and the closer Leo came to her, the more he could see that she was on the verge of tears.

"Miss Hall, you are upset. Come, we shall take the air on the terrace." She did not argue, merely allowed him to lead her from the room and out into the cooling night ambiance.

The terrace housed several groups, all animatedly talking, and all who looked in their direction and raised interested, surprised brows at them both.

Leo threw a displeased glance and moved Miss Hall out of their hearing. "What has happened?" he asked.

She sniffed, dabbing at her cheeks. Leo swallowed, fisting his hands at his sides. He'd never seen a woman cry, and he had the odd yet overwhelming urge to take her in his arms and comfort her.

The poor young woman had not had the best day. Lord Spencer first accosted her in the park for money, and now she was crying at a ball. Whatever next!

"I'm a pariah, my lord. I think it is better that you do not try to help me be anything else before you're shunned by society, too."

"They would not dare shun a future duke or a gentleman who hosts the best entertainments in London, if not England itself." His words did little to make her less upset, and he fought to think of what else he could say to make her happy. To see her smile.

"I do think your brother's gambling debts are hurting your chances. People do not know how much you're worth, as crass as such a conversation is with a gentlewoman."

She scoffed and rolled her eyes. "I'm no gentlewoman. I've merely been thrust into the society by chance."

Even so, some people will think that what your brother is spending is adding up, and you're not worth their trouble without a fortune."

She stared at him, her mouth agape and hurt in her blue eyes. "Are you trying to make me feel better or worse?" she asked him.

"No," he cursed himself a fool for possibly making the night more spoiled for her. "I'm trying to say that they do not know you. They're shallow enough to put worth on wealth, not a person's character. You're priceless to me." Even though he had not known her long, he already knew that to be true. She was a gem among the paste surrounding them, and they were all fools if they could not see past their lofty ideals.

"Well, I'm worth many thousands of pounds, thirty to be exact, so it would take a great debt for my brother to make me lose it. Not that I'm obligated to pay his way," she reminded him.

Leo stared at Miss Hall for several heartbeats, unable to comprehend that she was worth so much. He had thought three or five thousand pounds, but thirty...

Blazes.

The *ton* had to be unaware of this fact, or they would have banged down Lord and Lady Lupton-Gage's door years ago. "Who knows how much you're worth?" he asked.

She lifted her finger, pointing it at him. "No, you will not secretly or otherwise tell a soul how much I'm worth. I want a love match, and you agreed to help me find one. I think you'll be enough to make gentlemen interested. You'll just have to show more interest, not less at balls and dinners, so the *ton* marks your interest. I was alone most of the evening." She stared at him, taking in his every feature, and he could see she was debating his person. "Where were you anyway? Why so late to arrive?"

"I was at White's, if you must know. I had dinner there and caught up with several friends before coming to the Jenkins' ball. If I had known you were as alone as you were, I would have come sooner, and I shall endeavor to do so from now on."

Without thought, he touched her cheek, forgetting where they were. "I'll be sure to be here on time next time and will not leave you alone. I promised to help you, and I will. I'm sorry."

She smiled at him, and something within his chest

jerked pleasantly. However, he could not say what that was, nor did he want to right at this moment, not when it made him long for things he'd never wanted.

A rabella started at Lord Wyndham's touch. His hand was large and warm, and it took all her effort not to lean into his palm and rub against him like a cat seeking a pat.

She couldn't dare to dream of winning him, but that did not mean she could not enjoy the flirtation that was to commence when he helped her gain popularity.

If she gained popularity. That was yet to be determined. Even with them both being seen together, it had done little to make her more alluring to the opposite sex.

No one this evening had asked her to dance or be included in conversation. Even so, she would keep her hopes up and fight to forget the negative things that had befallen her since her brother's arrival in town and the problems that followed him here.

As if realizing what he was doing, Lord Wyndham ripped his hand away and shoved both into the pockets of his superfine coat, rocking back on his heels as if he were also standing too close to her.

"Come, let us return to the ball. I shall dance a waltz with you and commence our arrangement in truth this very night. No one will leave not surmising that I'm courting you. They will soon know you are a favorite of Marquess Wyndham, future Duke Carnavon. The *ton* will devour and fall over themselves to gain an audience with you."

"You're a good man, far better than I thought when first meeting you." She paused, sliding her arm within his as they walked toward the terrace doors. "Will you continue your scandalous parties, my lord?" She met his eyes and noted his slight frown of confusion. "I only ask," she continued, "because if you do, they will not think your intentions are true. They will think you're playing with me if you're still having your wild soirées."

"Hmm, yes, I see your point." They returned to the ballroom, and he led her onto the floor. "I shall be discreet *if* I host any entertainments at all. But I shall not be late for another ball. Merely let me know how many you require."

"You're being too kind. I do not know you or deserve it. Not after I tried to steal into your home and steal my brother's vowel of debt."

"I've never been a man who enjoys seeing women be taken for granted and used as you seem to be. And after what happened in the park, well, that disgraceful act I shall not allow to happen again."

A warm, comforting feeling swamped her at his kind words, and she could not hold back the little grin of delight that he was her friend, if she were so bold to think.

"A woman who is desperate enough to steal into my London town house in the middle of one of my parties is a woman in need of help. I could not turn you away without offering my services. I may be a cad, a rake, and rogue even, but I'm not cruel." He leaned close, ensuring privacy. "I merely allow the *ton* to think I am those things." His teasing grin made her laugh. The man was too charming for his own good.

"Well, I thank you, my lord. For everything you're doing for me. I'm most appreciative."

"Call me Leo. We're courting, are we not? Should we not be on such intimate terms?"

Arabella took a calming breath, stilling her heart and willing it not to jump out of her chest. "Very well, Leo," she said, testing his name on her lips for the first time and liking how it sounded. "You may call me Arabella when we're alone."

He watched her, his eyes swirling with mystery that she doubted she would ever know or understand. "Arabella, a pretty name for a pretty face," he quipped.

Oh dear, there went her heart once again.

Calm yourself, Arabella, it is not real.

And yet she could dream. If only for a Season.

CHAPTER
NINE

Damn, she was a pretty lass, and the moment he heard her name, something within him twisted and turned, made him feel like he needed to move faster, think clearer, stop acting the lout all his life, and settle.

But this was a deal. A farce. A way to ensure she married and married well. And he would remain within the *ton* and ensure that occurred for the delightful Arabella Hall.

How could he allow anything else to befall her? She was agreeable, young, beautiful, and an heiress. What was not to like or deem worthy?

That she spoke to him even knowing the parties he held, having been at one herself, and still thought him worthy as a friend, was not what he thought possible from a debutante.

Perhaps they made the women more open-minded in Brighton.

He pulled her into his arms and reveled in the feel of her silk gown swaying with each step, her trim waist that his hand wanted to caress and squeeze. Her breasts were perfect. She was flawless.

Stop, Leo. She's not one of your paramours...

Nor could he try to seduce her. She was a maid and would be married soon to a respectable fellow. He could not seduce her even if he thought she would make a fine little bed mate.

"Lord Bankes has been watching us since we returned from the terrace. Do you think perhaps that he may find me intriguing enough to ask me to dance?"

When the dance allowed, Leo glanced toward Lord Bankes, who stood talking to Lord Lupton-Gage. He narrowed his eyes, taking in the young man. He was just a boy, one and twenty, he believed, and from a good family in Hampshire.

"Well, that he is speaking to your guardian is surely a good sign, and I have no information on his lordship that would make me not agree for him to call on you." Arabella studied the young man when he swung her about, her eyes widening with interest. "He is handsome, even if he is very young."

"You're forgetting that you are young," he reminded her, watching as she bit her lip in thought. He tore his gaze away, looking over her head and anywhere else but her mouth. He may have to keep his parties to a minimum while he was pretending to court Miss Hall, but he would need to relieve himself sexually and soon if he were to survive the next several weeks.

The lady in his arms was far too alluring, especially for a virginal miss.

Leo, Miss Hall would be as still as a wooden plank in bed.

He almost scoffed at his thoughts. He couldn't see that as being true. She was bold. He knew that after she arrived at his home, uninvited and tried to steal from him. No, she would not be meek and mild when passion blazed through her. Indeed not. She would be all fire, adventurous, and a vixen, is what she would be.

"How old are you, my lord?" she asked him, pulling him from thoughts of them tumbling over his bed and enjoying each other for hours. "I, ahh, I'm eight and twenty. Too old for you, Arabella," he teased.

His gaze dipped to her lips, and he instinctively pulled her closer. Her breasts brushed his waistcoat and he swallowed. Hard. Damn it, he should not have done that. Her little startled gasp opened her mouth, and all thoughts of devouring her bombarded his mind.

What the hell was wrong with him? He was to help her. Not seduce her.

She rallied and met his eyes defiantly. "You're not too old for me, Leo, but I know you're also not for me. I know you do not intend to marry. You wish to relish your bachelorhood, so your assistance and friendship are enough for me."

"So we're becoming friends then," he teased, knowing he wanted that most of all, no matter what happened between them.

"I hope we are. I do not have many, and so what a boon to have a future duke as one. I shall make everyone green with envy and give them much to talk about... How a house servant came to be friends with the upper echelon of society."

"You are no longer a housemaid, Arabella. Do not say such things anymore. You're a lady, a woman of means, and with connections that place you equal to those in this room. Do not let anyone say otherwise to you."

"You're very sweet, do you know that? I did not think

you would be the first time we met, but you're lovely under your hard, roguish exterior."

A rabella could have swallowed her tongue at her words.

Lovely!

What had she been thinking to state such a thought aloud? Perhaps the ratafia had been spiked, and she was a little foxed to be so fluid with her words.

Not that Lord Wyndham seemed to mind. He threw back his head, laughed, and pulled her into a spin that left her reeling.

"Well, you're lovely too, my friend." He met her eyes. His dark, penetrating gaze made her want to forget all the other men in the room, in London for that matter, and only dream of the man in her arms.

When had she started to dream of him as her husband? Not that he ever would be. She would have to work hard and learn to enjoy another man's company as much as she enjoyed Leo's if she were to have a successful marriage.

The dance came to an unfortunate end, and she waltzed to a stop not far from Lord and Lady Lupton-Gage. Reign gestured for her to join them, and she made her way over, rallying herself for the introduction to Lord Bankes.

Surprisingly, Lord Wyndham followed, towering at her back, and the closer she came to her party, the wider Lord Bankes's eyes grew.

"Arabella, may I introduce you to Lord Bankes. Lord Bankes, this is my cousin, Miss Arabella Hall," Reign said, her cousin's gaze moving to Lord Wyndham at her back. "And Lord Wyndham, of course, how are you this evening?"

"Very well, thank you, Lady Lupton-Gage."

Lord Lupton-Gage held his hand out to Leo and shook it before they moved to one side to speak. "It's lovely to meet you, Lord Bankes. I hear you're from Hampshire. A lovely part of England, is it not? Known for its vast forests, if I'm not mistaken?"

"It is indeed, Miss Hall, how very astute that you would know that." He smiled warmly, and Arabella had to agree that he was a handsome man, but as young as she feared. This close to his lordship, she could see he sported very little facial hair. In fact, it did not look like he shaved at all.

Lord Wyndham seemed to always have a shadow on his jaw, which gave him an edge of mystery and danger.

Her stomach fluttered at the thought of Leo, and it took all her self-control not to glance in his direction.

Get yourself together, Arabella, before he thinks you like him more than a friend and runs for the hills.

"I like to read, my lord. I must have encountered that little tidbit of information at some time."

He gestured toward the ballroom floor. "Would you care to dance? I believe a country dance is next?"

"I would like that very much, thank you," she agreed, linking her arm in his and letting him lead her toward the ballroom floor. Arabella caught sight of Reign and her delight at her new dance partner.

He was a lovely gentleman and one she ought to consider. She would try harder to be more herself, learn more about him, and see if they would suit. Try to stop thinking of the man whose attention burned a line down her back, warming her even from afar.

Lord Wyndham's.

CHAPTER
TEN

L eo spoke to Lord Lupton-Gage, a gentleman he'd known for many years, even if he'd rarely stepped foot at a *tonnish* event the past few Seasons.

But now, listening to his lordship speak of his oldest child and the little boy's ability to ride a miniature pony had him debating his choices.

Lupton-Gage made it all sound so charming, and yet, before this evening, he'd never once thought of children as lovely. More like bothersome, messy, loud little creatures who one left with the nanny as much as possible.

His father had a lot to answer for, being the atrocious parent he was.

He caught a glimpse of Arabella dancing a scotch reel with Lord Bankes. She appeared happy, engaged with his lordship's conversation, yet her eyes did not sparkle as much as he'd seen them do in the past.

Was she happy? Perhaps on closer inspection, his lordship wasn't as entertaining or exciting as she'd hoped.

But, the Season was young, and there would be more gentlemen, he would ensure there were. Ones who did not seek her fortune but sought her heart as the main requirement.

The dance ended, and Lord Bankes walked her over to where a footman held a tray of lemonade. She gladly took a glass and sipped, a small smile on her lips as his lordship talked.

"Wyndham, do not tell me you're interested in my wife's cousin? Rumor has it that you're against the notion of marriage. Am I to assume that you've changed your mind after meeting Miss Hall?"

Lupton-Gage's words pulled him from his interest in Arabella. "No, I have not changed my mind, but I have agreed, as her friend, to help her find a gentleman worthy of her. Do you know Lord Spencer accosted her in Grosvenor Square just yesterday and notified her of where she could send the funds to pay for her brother's gambling debt to him?"

To his credit, Lupton-Gage visually reined in the temper that flittered across his visage before he answered, "He did what? Arabella did not mention this to me, only of her brother's habits, which I'm happy to say will be dealt with soon. He's to leave for my country estate within the week."

"Yes, it seems to be happening often at balls and parties. I suppose she did not want to worry you, but I over-heard Lord Spencer's conversation yesterday, and I gave him a good set down for it, and that is why I thought to help her in society, be a guide, and not allow her to be fooled by these young bucks." That was not entirely true. After meeting her at his house and seeing the desperation she harbored to protect herself and her sibling, he could only do the right thing by her and help. If only once in his life.

Not that Lupton-Gage needed to know where they met and under what circumstances.

"You do not have to do that for Miss Hall, but I do thank you for your assistance so far. I can only assume her dancing with Lord Bankes was at your urging."

"To his credit, his interest was his own, but I encouraged her to be open-minded toward him. He's a good man, new to London, and not interested in whoring as so many young gentlemen are."

Lupton-Gage cleared his throat, and his lips twitched. No doubt well aware of Leo's reputation. "Well, there could be a reason for his lack of feminine connections when it comes to Lord Bankes."

Leo frowned. "Really, what do you mean?" He looked back to Arabella and his lordship and noted she now looked as bored as he had been when he was a guest at an event he did not enjoy.

Damn, he supposed he'd have to look elsewhere for another gentleman if that was how it was going.

"Lord Bankes is rumored to enjoy the company of his own sex, over that of the opposite, if you understand my meaning."

Leo winced. His attention moved to those near where Arabella stood, and dread settled in his stomach. Groups of debutantes stared at Arabella and giggled, whispered behind their fans, and grinned as if they knew a secret she did not.

Had he inadvertently made an error and pushed her toward a gentleman everyone knew wasn't interested in women, not in the way Leo or any hot-blooded male was interested in women?

Had he made her even more of a pariah, an amusement that the *ton* could ridicule and exclude?

"I did not know that. How I missed this information is beyond me, but I shall rectify it posthaste." Without waiting for Lupton-Gage to reply, he moved toward Arabella, determined to rescue her from further ostracizing.

R elief poured through her at the sight of Lord Wyndham pushing his way through the crowd of guests toward her. Was he going to wish her a goodnight and leave?

Please do not leave me with Lord Bankes.

Never in her life had she ever encountered such a tedious conversation, and that was when she spent the majority of her nights alone at parties, talking to Reign or Evie when she had been here, never anyone else.

"Miss Hall, Lady Lupton-Gage wishes you to return to her."

Arabella looked to where Reign stood and noted she was talking with the Duchess of Romney and not at all bothered where she was.

Even so, if it meant that she could escape Lord Bankes, who was a kind gentleman but not the one to win her heart, unfortunately, she would go with his lordship.

"Of course, if she insists."

"She does." Lord Wyndham held out his hand.

"Thank you for the dance, my lord. I hope to see you again."

"Indeed you will, Miss Hall," he said, striding away from them without a backward glance.

"Thank you," she whispered as soon as they were far enough away from anyone overhearing their conversation. "I do not think Lord Bankes will suit."

"No, I do not think that he will either."

Arabella pushed down the hope that rose within her that his agreement was due to his interest. She should not get ahead of herself. His words could mean nothing other than a friend who had noted her boredom and had taken heed.

"Why do you agree with me? I have not told you my reasons why."

Lord Wyndham pulled her toward the side of the room near a partially open window. They stood apart from other guests, hidden slightly by some potted palms. "Because I have been informed that Bankes is inappropriate, and that is all I'll say on the matter. To say any more would be ungentlemanly of me."

She scoffed before she could stop herself. "You're not worried about being ungentlemanly or inappropriate. Do be serious and tell me, Leo. No one will know what you say. Your secret will be safe with me," she teased.

He let out a sigh and met her eyes. "Lord Bankes appears to like men above women, if you understand my meaning."

Arabella gaped, having never known such a thing was possible. Did that go for women also? She supposed it could...

"Do you mean he would not want to kiss me, do his husbandly duties with me should we marry?"

Leo cleared his throat and pulled at his cravat. "It does not matter what he would not do. You're not entertaining his interest a moment longer, so it does not signify."

"Tell me, Leo, what you mean." Arabella needed to know. To be ignorant was too irritating to mention.

He met her eyes. His deep, green gaze swirled with an emotion she could not read, but her body recognized. Heat prickled over her skin, her stomach fluttered, and she swallowed a squeak of alarm.

"It means that he would not fuck you as you ought to be fucked when married. It means that he would not touch you, tease your sweet, untutored flesh, or kiss you wildly, passionately, so much so that you are left breathless, grappling for purchase. You would not be bedded as a man ought to bed a woman so they are satisfied, blissful, and looking for more."

Oh dear God, had Leo said those things aloud?

She shut her mouth with a snap, fighting the urge to ask him if he bedded women so. Who was she kidding? Of course he did, and the thought ripped jealousy through her like a knife.

"Is that how you make love to a woman?" The words slipped from her, a whisper between them.

His cocky, wolfish grin was back and she knew her answer before he replied. "I don't make love, Arabella. I fuck. But yes, that's exactly what I do. Every. Delicious. Time."

CHAPTER

ELEVEN

L ater that evening, Arabella knocked on the door to the private parlor upstairs used by Lady Lupton-Gage and was relieved when she heard Reign bid her enter.

She shut the door as soon as she entered the room, glad to see that his lordship wasn't present.

"Arabella, well, this is a surprise. I thought you had gone to bed when we returned from the ball."

Arabella sat on a settee across from Reign, needing to speak to her alone, woman to woman, with no one about to interrupt her words. They would be difficult enough to voice. "I did try," she admitted. "But I could not sleep. I need to tell you something I'm doing in London so you shall not be alarmed or believe there is hope when there is none in truth."

Reign frowned and placed down the needlework she was sewing. "Well, that does sound ominous. Should I be worried before you tell me whatever has been bothering you?"

"No, I do not think so." But in truth, Arabella was not so

sure it wasn't alarming what she was about with Lord Wyndham. He was a rogue, after all, and one determined not to marry. Should she accidentally place herself in a compromising position with him, as innocent as that may be, he would be forced to ask for her hand.

But would he offer? Save her reputation? Something told her he would not.

Her ladyship let out a small sound of derision. "Very well, I think it is best to tell me and let me decide whether you're correct in that estimation."

Arabella took a calming breath and rallied her thoughts together. "Lord Wyndham is helping me in society. He came across me being bothered in the park the other day," she explained how it all came about. "I think he feels sorry for me but wants to help in any case, and I agreed to allow him to."

"So you're going to allow his lordship, a man known to throw the most scandalous parties in London, to escort you to balls and parties to make you more popular with the young men in London."

"Yes, and help me with Frederick. He's letting everyone he knows know they should not allow him to gamble, as his sister is no longer paying his way."

"Well." Reign let out a deep breath and sat back into the chaise longue. "It is honorable that his lordship is willing to escort you about. He is right that it will entice gentlemen who may not have considered you, that if you've caught the eye of the future Duke Carnavon, they may be overlooking something they should not. But I'm more relieved that he is helping with Frederick. I know how worried you've been regarding his behavior."

"It's been a terrible worry after yesterday's episode at

the park. I have never wished for the ground to open and swallow me whole before, but yesterday was the first."

"I can imagine." Reign watched her a moment before she said, "Are you friends with Lord Wyndham then?"

Arabella thought about it a moment and nodded. "I believe we are. He readily admits that he's a rogue and not willing to marry. He says that by helping me, the mamas of the *ton* will leave him alone, and so far, they have. It is kind, do you not think, that he would help me? Not that I want anyone to feel sorry for me, but if our little arrangement means that I could find my future husband, a man who loves me as much as I hope to love him, well, all the better."

"Not to mention that Lord Wyndham is a very handsome man. Tall, athletic, rides a horse well..." Reign's words trailed off, and her brows raised. "Do you wish the man who wins your heart to look similar to Lord Wyndham? You would not be the only debutante in town to hope such things."

Heat kissed her cheeks, and she glanced down at her hands in her lap, unsure if she should admit to all she had felt for his lordship. Somehow, saying it aloud meant that it was out there in the universe, spoken, a truth of sorts, never to be a secret again.

"He would not look at me, even if I harbor such fanciful thoughts."

"He is helping you. That is more than he has offered any debutante ever. He is not the kind of man who enters society, prefers to keep to the edges and only look in now and then." Reign paused, her fingers tapping her needlework in contemplation. "Perhaps you have tweaked his curiosity enough that he is having a Season with you but is unaware of what his subconscious mind has done."

Arabella laughed, unable to imagine such things. Lord

Wyndham, subconsciously interested in her? The idea was preposterous. "No, he merely felt sorry for a wallflower, a woman who was once a housemaid and wished to stop me from having a second disastrous Season."

"You may be wrong. I watched him this evening, and he, in turn, observed you the entire time you were dancing with Lord Bankes. His interest is piqued, even if you do not believe me, and you ought to use that to your advantage."

"How?" she asked, leaning forward in her chair.

"Well, I think you ought to do as he instructs. Dance with the men he believes to be honorable and worthy of your hand, and he would know. Anyone who does not frequent his home would be respectable." Reign winked and chuckled at her words. "Mayhap, by doing so, you will make him jealous. A notion that I know would be foreign to him and perhaps one he does not recognize at first, but if he does like you more than even he knows, play his game and test the theory."

"I couldn't be so bold as to hope, nevertheless to be coy, fashionable, and elegant in front of him. I do not have the fine graces everyone else seems to have in spades. I do try, but they have been taught how to talk, walk, eat, and smile since birth. I've only had such learnings for three years."

Reign's lips smoothed into a displeased smile. "You are just as fashionable as everyone else, and tomorrow, we shall go and purchase all new gowns. Dresses, shoes, bonnets, and gloves that will set any marquess and future duke's heart on fire. If my plan works, adjacent to yours with his lordship, you shall marry a man I believe already makes your heart beat fast. Am I right?" she asked.

Arabella could not lie to Reign. She swallowed her nerves at admitting to such a thing aloud. "I do like him more than I should. I know he's only helping me out of the goodness of his rogue heart, but that makes me only like him more. I'm a fool."

Reign waved her finger at her. "Oh no, you're no fool, Arabella, and I think that given enough time together, Lord Wyndham will come to learn how marvelous you are, sweet and kind, even with your humble beginnings. I think he shall fall in love with you."

"I think you may have had too much champagne this evening, Reign, but thank you for your kind words, for everything, but can I win him to my side? I would not know where to start."

"Start by being yourself as you have been. We shall purchase a new wardrobe of the highest fashion, and with a little flirtation, a coquettish glance here and there, a stolen touch, I think you shall have all that your heart desires."

Hope thrummed through her, and she bit her lip, daring to dream of such an ideal outcome. "Do you think he will give up his roguish lifestyle for me? Being married seems so much duller than attending the scandalous parties he's renowned for."

"You know what they say, my dear," Reign said, again picking up her needlework.

"What is that?" she asked.

"That reformed rakes make the best husbands." She glanced at her. "And I should know. I married one."

CHAPTER
TWELVE

L eo had compiled a list of fitting suitors for Arabella and would introduce them to her this evening at the Frost ball. She would also be happy to hear that he had been sent a missive from Duke Blackhaven, who had informed him that Mr. Frederick Hall had been refused entry to the duke's gambling hell.

It was a good turn of events for Arabella, who did not need her brother's bad behavior to impact her Season more than it already had.

Leo waited for her at the ball, sipping his smooth brandy and conversing with a few of the gentlemen as he stood to the side, taking in the many guests who flocked to the ballroom for a night of revelry.

He took a deep breath, pushing down the boredom he had always encountered at such entertainment. He was to have one of his private events at home in several days, one he had not told Miss Hall of as yet.

Would she be disappointed in him that he was to host one of his scandalous parties? He had promised to be discreet, possibly not hold any until after she was married.

But this was his annual masked ball. He could not cancel it now, not when so many of his friends and the *ton*, some of them present here this evening, looked forward to the night each year.

A night that promised secrecy, revelry, and opportunities to enjoy the opposite sex without shame or scandal.

A spark of affability coursed through him at the sight of Arabella, along with an emotion he had not sensed before.

Shock? No, he shook his head. That was not it. Surprise? Hmm, no, not that either.

Awe...

He swallowed. Hard.

What was she wearing? Did Lady Lupton-Gage know what she had slipped on before coming to the ball this evening? He frowned. Surely, she would have...

The gown of the deepest pink suited Arabella's dark hair and perfectly creamy skin. She wore no jewels, not that she needed any. The empire-style gown slipped over her, falling from her ample breasts and pulling more than just his attention.

Her hair sat atop her head in a motif of curls, accentuating her high cheekbones and bright eyes that shone like sapphires in the candlelight.

Blast it all to hell. She was magnificent.

He schooled his features when she caught sight of him, a warm, friendly smile twisting her luscious lips that had the smallest amount of rouge upon them.

He downed the last of his brandy and placed the glass on a nearby mantel. When Arabella stood before him, he bowed over her hand and dragged her onto the dance floor.

He had to dance with her. Hold her in his arms. Marvel at her beauty close enough to ogle to his heart's content. Of course, he did not want a wife, but that did not mean he could not admire a woman who wanted a husband. Hold her in his arms until she became another's.

He clenched his jaw at the thought. Fought not to voice words he never wanted to utter. Words like the gentlemen he had chosen for Miss Hall were no longer suitable. That she would never be satisfied with them.

Why, Leo? Are you thinking she would only be satisfied with you?

"You look...breathtaking, Miss Hall," he uttered finally.

She met his gaze, tipping up her face with a pleased countenance that was hard to ignore. "Why thank you, Lord Wyndham. I thought I should assist you in helping me find a husband. New gowns were required. Do you like what I'm wearing?" she boldly asked.

He cleared his throat, fighting not to stare at her breasts that the empire-style gown seemed to accentuate more than any of her other dresses had in the past.

He closed his eyes a moment. The image of his mouth covering one of her puckered, rosy nipples, suckling her, teasing her with his tongue, bombarded his mind.

His cock twitched, and he fought not to drag her from the ballroom floor and show her just how much he liked her gown. Preferably off her body.

"Very much so," he answered. "You will be quite the favored debutante, I should imagine, this evening. Especially with my interest still on show for all the *ton*."

"You're a good friend. I cannot thank you enough." She smiled at him, and his heart skipped a beat. A friend? He almost scoffed at the term. The thoughts that were going through his mind at present were far from friendly. No one did the things he was imagining to their friend.

When had she morphed into a stunning beauty who took his breath away?

. . .

Arabella took a calming breath and fought to keep her composure. She had never seen a man look at her with hunger, but something swirled in Lord Wyndham's eyes that gave her hope that what Reign had said the night before may come to fruition.

He watched her with an intentness that had not been there before. His gaze often slipped over her person and left her breathless, as if his hands had followed his gaze and touched her flesh.

Suppose she played her cards right, kept her interest in him a secret and allowed any of the gentlemen his lordship suggested to court her. It may pique his interest.

Maybe he would want her for himself.

She could only hope, but even if he did not, she might find a kind man who loved her, if she were fortunate. No matter what happened this Season, something told her Lord Wyndham would not disappoint her.

"I have compiled a list of four gentlemen I believe would suit you. They are all upstanding, none frequent my entertainments, and they do not gamble or mistreat women. I think you shall have a difficult time choosing between them, as a matter of fact."

"Is that so?" she said in a teasing note. "Well, I shall determine if that is true, but in all seriousness, I shall try to find a husband from whomever you recommend. I know you do not need to be helping me, which only tells me you have no hidden motive."

"Of course not. Other than the guilt I harbor after winning against your brother and finding out you would pay the debt, I know I do not owe you anything. But it does not hurt to be kind or generous."

Arabella chuckled. "I do not believe that for a second. You are not an awful man all the time. You may be a little scandalous with your parties, but that is nothing serious. No matter what you do, women would still wish to marry you."

"Not if they knew that I would not give up my vices no matter how much I may care for them."

His words gave her pause, and she schooled her features, not wanting him to see that his words disappointed her. "Are you saying you would not be faithful if you were to marry?"

"I will never marry, but should I find myself in a misfortunate position, then no, I would not be faithful. No one can last a lifetime and desire or crave the same person forever. That is not realistic. You must see that."

Arabella bit her lip. The conversation was inappropriate, certainly not for a debutante, and still, she wanted to hear more. Know what he meant. "For a woman, we do not have a choice but to be faithful, or we would be shunned from society. Our children rumored as bastards," she whispered in truth, to keep others from hearing their words.

"Which is why I shall never place a woman in such a position as to be my wife. It would be unfair and cruel."

The hope she had harbored evaporated and died at his declaration. So, he was truly determined on his course of bachelorhood forever. "But what if you fall in love, Leo?"

He stared at her, his attention dipping to her lips. Arabella felt the breath in her lungs seize when he dipped his head. Was he going to kiss her? Here and now, in the middle of a ball?

Instead, he leaned down, his words tickling her ear. "I do not believe in love either, Arabella."

She shivered despite his words before the dance ended,

and he twirled her to a stop. "Would you like an introduction to Lord Mansfield? He's first on my list for you."

Arabella rallied, forcing a smile on her lips that felt awkward and wrong. "Indeed, please do. I look forward to it," she lied, wanting to skulk away to the retiring room instead, where she could wallow in her delusions of having Lord Leo Wyndham fall in love with her and marry her.

Foolish chit that she was.

CHAPTER
THIRTEEN

L eo made the introduction to Arabella and watched as Lord Mansfield fumbled over his words, trying to make a good impression. There were good men out there for Miss Hall. She had perhaps been missing some of them due to her nervousness regarding her past.

Not that anyone looking at her right now for one minute could believe she had once been a housemaid.

Never had a woman caught his eye as much as Arabella did this evening, so naturally beautiful, her long lashes blinking demurely as she spoke with his lordship. She certainly knew how to play the game of courtship, no matter her misgivings on the notion at present.

She laughed at something Lord Mansfield said, and her attention moved past his lordship to anchor on him. Leo's stomach knotted, swirling with an emotion he had never felt.

Lord Mansfield's laughter cut into thoughts he ought not to be having. Thoughts such as imaginings of her leaning up to kiss him, of having her dark-blue eyes glisten with need and desire, with demands he would only be too happy to meet.

He clamped his jaw shut, looking elsewhere and ignoring Miss Hall as best he could. But still, he could hear their benign conversation that spoke of minor importance, and he could not have been more bored in his life.

Was Arabella bored, too? She did not sound like it, but upon closer inspection of Lord Mansfield, his overeagerness for his dogs was too much to stomach, even for Leo.

And he liked dogs.

"Would you care for a lemonade, Miss Hall? I can fetch you one if you like."

"That would be most welcome, my lord," she answered before Lord Mansfield ran off to fetch his good deed for the day.

Dear Lord in heaven, she could not marry that cold fish.

"Well, he is a charming man. I thank you for the introduction." Miss Hall watched Lord Mansfield move toward a footman, who held a tray of crystal glasses.

Leo frowned, trying to decide if she were in earnest. "Do you not think that he's a little, well, how should I say this... dull?"

"Dull? Whyever would you say such a thing? He's interested in reading and riding horses, just as I am. He's only two and twenty and, as you said, from a good family." She paused before meeting his eyes. "His grandfather was in trade, so I suppose we have a little more in common than you and I do. Your family has held the ducal title for how many years?" she questioned him.

"Several hundred, but I fail to see how that makes you have more in common with him than with me."

"What does it matter, so long as I have a little in common with him." She threw him a slight grin that he wasn't entirely sure was innocent. "You have sworn off marriage and agreed to help me, so you cannot back down now, even if you are finding the process tedious and not to your liking."

"I never said it wasn't to my liking. I just do not wish for you to make a mistake, and I feel that continuing the courtship with Lord Mansfield would be. Why not consider my next gentleman? Lord Olivier. He's a baron from Surrey and the most-sought-after this Season, but he hasn't shown much interest in the fashionable elite. He appears to enjoy bookish ladies more."

Leo glanced about the room, searching for his next gentleman for Arabella. He frowned, disappointed when he could not spot him.

"Leo," he heard her quietly say. "For a man who does not partake in society often, you know a lot about these men. Care to enlighten me on that ability, if you please?"

Again, he met her gaze and marveled at her loveliness this evening. She was striking, a goddess, and he was surprised no gentlemen had not already stolen her for a dance.

He certainly wanted to. In fact, for the first time in his life, he felt like a bumbling fool who did not know what to say next.

"I had my steward look into who would suit you." He paused to recount how he came to know who would suit Miss Hall. Was he too invested in her? Did he care?

Blast it all to hell. He was a rogue, a rake, a libertine. The idea of playing matchmaker did not sit well with him, but he could not ignore his outrage watching her be accosted in the park. The light in her eyes dimmed the more Lord Spencer spoke of her brother's debt that he expected her to pay.

No, he could not leave her to the wolves. He would protect her, his one good deed in his life, see her happily married and continue with his wayward lifestyle when she was settled.

A rabella heard a deep, smooth voice to her side and turned to find Lord Russell, a gentleman who had never paid her any heed before, bowing before her.

"Miss Hall, Lord Wyndham, good evening to you both." He turned to her, a small, welcoming smile on his lips. "Would you care to dance, Miss Hall? There is to be a waltz next, and I simply must have this dance."

Arabella took his hand without hesitation and allowed the earl to lead her onto the dance floor. The orchestra started the first notes of the waltz, and she was soon gliding about the ballroom floor with a man who was as handsome and intimidating as Lord Wyndham.

It was an exciting turn of events, and she wondered if she could use Lord Russell to her advantage. Would Leo be jealous? Try to steer her away from the earl for being too similar to his own.

The idea of such a husband was tempting, but after seeing Lord Wyndham's sweet, caring side, she wanted him and no one else. Not that she would admit to such thinking, but it was as accurate as she was dancing in Lord Russell's arms.

Her heart had been touched, and nothing else would do.

"I must apologize, Miss Hall, for not dancing with you before this evening. I have many demands on my time, but seeing you this evening, I could not deny myself a moment longer from your glittering sphere."

Arabella raised her brow. Such poetic words from a man who had not looked at her once, not even in passing before this night.

Not that she wanted Lord Russell, but she would certainly use him for a little flirtation and enjoyment. Rumor had it that he was besotted with the widow Lady Southwell. Perhaps he, too, was using her to test her ladyship's commitment not to marry again.

Perhaps they could come to an agreement, too...

"Lord Russell, you flatter me, but are you not courting Lady Southwell? I'm certain I heard that you were on the brink of asking her to marry you. Why are you dancing with me, my lord?"

He gaped, surprise rippling over his handsome features before he succumbed to her knowledge. "So you have heard the rumors, too. They are only that, Miss Hall. Rumors."

"But are they not true?" Arabella caught sight of Lady Southwell watching them, and her thin, displeased mouth bore her disappointment at seeing his lordship dancing with her. "Perhaps you ought to keep pretending to court me. It may spark jealousy in Lady Southwell, and she may change her mind. She certainly looks displeased right at this moment."

"She does?" he barked, a mistake, clearly, if his horrified expression was anything to go by. "My apologies, Miss Hall. How you must loathe me."

"No, not at all. We're all playing a game in this society, myself included, but mayhap we could be of service to each other."

He watched her, interest in her this time, not Lady Southwell. "Whatever do you mean?" he asked.

"Well, I, too, am trying to convince someone that I'm worthy, and so if we spark up a friendship and dance at balls and parties, it's sure to make the ones who are being difficult possibly realize they're on the brink of losing what they want."

Lord Russell glanced over her shoulder, and his eyes darkened in the stormy, needy way Lord Wyndham's did when she sometimes caught him looking at her. "Lady Southwell does look displeased by our dance. You may be on to something with this madcap idea of yours, Miss Hall."

"But it must remain a secret. No one can ever know," she urged, knowing that if Leo found out about her scheming, it would only send him running for the hills and as far away from her as possible.

"A secret between new friends. I like it," he agreed.

"I do, too," she answered, throwing herself into the dance more than she ever would have before. They had respective potential spouses to make jealous. One ought to be dedicated to the art of love warfare.

FOURTEEN

The following evening, Leo arrived at the Delaney ball only to find Miss Hall in the arms of Lord Russell, dancing a cotillion, engaged and laughing at each other's words as if no one else existed in the room.

A knot of unease settled in his stomach, and he schooled his features, bidding the hosts, Lord and Lady Delaney a good evening before working his way through the throng of guests.

By the time he reached the ballroom's end, he had caught Miss Hall being escorted out onto the terrace, lemonade in hand, and talking animatedly with Lord Russell.

Leo ground his teeth. The man was as bad as he was when it came to his whoring. Whatever was she doing, allowing such a cad to court her? He was certainly not on his list of eligible gentlemen he had found for her.

He followed and was glad he did so when he caught them both starting toward the darkened gardens.

"Lord Russell, Lord and Lady Delaney wished for a

word. They mentioned it upon my arrival and charged me with finding you," he lied.

Lord Russell bent over Miss Hall's hand, kissing her gloved fingers and throwing her a look that made Leo's temper sour.

What the hell was the blackguard thinking, trying to seduce her in front of anyone? The man had no shame.

He watched Arabella as Lord Russell strode back indoors before her gaze finally landed on him and cooled a little. Leo fought the disappointment that stabbed at him at her reaction to his presence.

"Lord Russell," he started, "is not a gentleman I would recommend you allow courtship. He's attended many of my parties and would unlikely be a suitable, honorable husband."

"But he is so very handsome, Leo. Have you seen his jawline?" She sighed, biting her lip and sending his pulse to race. "I would like to touch his jaw and see if it is as cutting as it appears."

"I'm certain it is, and you'll only get sliced if you touch it, injured in other terms."

She grinned up at him, tipping her head to one side. "Oh, you're such a good friend to care for whom I allow to court me. I do hope we shall always have this friend-ship. You're so kind to me, Leo. How can I ever thank you?"

Leo led her down the stairs off the terrace and along the graveled path into the garden. "There is no need for thanks," he all but barked, cringing when she flinched a little at his harshness.

He sighed. "I apologize, Arabella. It has been a long day." He forgot to mention that the day had dragged frus-tratingly since he had not seen her since last evening. He had thought of little else but of her all day, and that in itself left him uneasy.

To think of one woman in particular was out of character for him, and he had decided that he would throw himself into his next private entertainment and fuck his thoughts back to how they had always been before Miss Hall came into his life.

He closed his eyes, even that rebellion leaving him less than enthusiastic.

What the hell was wrong with him?

"I think Lord Russell is delightful, and he's very attentive and handsome and a little bit naughty like yourself. I like him very much. Certainly not boring as you believed Lord Mansfield to be."

All true, of course, his words coming back to haunt him. "But do you not want someone reliable? Lord Russell has never been known to show interest in anyone but himself or the women who frequent my entertainment. He would not be faithful to you." He paused. "I thought you wanted a husband who loved you."

"Oh, I do," she agreed readily. "But there is no saying that he will not fall in love with me. I'm charming, am I not?" she teased, gifting him a teasing grin. "And I somehow charmed you into helping me."

"I was not charmed," he denied, even though a part of him certainly liked this lively, amusing side of Miss Hall. "I saw you in need, did not like what I saw, and thought to change it. That is very much different."

She waved his words aside, as if he had not spoken at all. "What if Lord Russell was going to kiss me in the gardens, and you stopped him by seeking me out and sending him on his way?"

Her words brought him to a stop, and he wrenched her

about, staring down at her and wondering where the woman in the park, the meek, beaten-down wallflower, had disappeared to. This woman was bold and determined to get what she wanted, even risking scandal, if he read her right. "You cannot mean you wanted to kiss him so soon. You could be ruined, forced to marry him without knowing him."

"I could get to know him well once we're married, and we do get along effortlessly, and that was but a day. Imagine a lifetime," Arabella paused. "I'm certain I could make him fall in love with me."

Leo swallowed, wondering when he had lost control of this situation, which left him at sixes and sevens. "I do not like it. You must be cautious."

Arabella glanced around the darkened garden and then back at Lord Wyndham. "Like now, my lord. Alone in a garden with one of London's most notorious rakes. Perhaps you should be cautious before you're forced to marry me instead."

He appeared to realize where they were and ushered them farther into the darkness. "We're friends. It's different between us."

She scoffed before she could think twice about doing so. "I doubt the upper ten thousand would think that nothing untoward is occurring merely because we're friends."

"But nothing untoward is occurring," he said, his voice a deep timbre she had never heard before. A tone that left her unsettled and wanting. She was not used to feeling two emotions, not before she met Lord Wyndham, in any case.

"We may know this, but no one else does. We must return to the ballroom before anyone sees us frolicking out in the dark gardens like two lovers. They may be used to finding your lordship in such circumstances, but I, most certainly not."

He sighed, and as they were about to start along the garden path, footsteps sounded, and voices of a woman and man Arabella did not recognize floated ever closer toward them.

Leo hauled her into his arms and stepped under a low-lying willow tree, shading her gown that illuminated in the moonlight with his body and superfine coat.

Through his shirt and waistcoat, Arabella could feel the beat of his racing heart, feel the heat of his skin. Sandalwood teased her senses, and she closed her eyes, reveling in the feel of him holding her against his body, enjoying his strength.

He smelled so good...

She wanted to slip her arms around his neck, meet his gaze, and ask for that first kiss she taunted him about with Lord Russell only minutes earlier.

But she did not.

He kept vigil over his shoulder, the couple's voices dimming as they walked farther into the gardens. A heartbeat or two, Arabella could not say; he tipped his head back to face her, his eyes flaring as he realized the position in which they now stood.

Time stood still.

The calm of the night did not even dare to intrude on this moment. Not even the music thought to float through the gardens. There was nothing but the two of them staring at each other, she in his arms, his hands metal bonds around her back, holding her in place.

He slid her down his body, her tiptoes finally hitting the lawns beneath her slippered feet. Still, he did not step back.

Instead, his eyes darkened with a hunger she had longed to be the recipient of. The longing burned in his gaze for her to take a chance, to be brave and reach for what she wanted.

Kiss him, Arabella.

Her attention dipped to his lips. His chest rose and fell in rapid succession, and before she could close the space between them, lean up, and take what she wanted, he pushed her away and strode from under the tree, leaving her alone in the garden and without the satisfaction of tasting him, if only once.

CHAPTER

FIFTEEN

L ike a coward, Leo hid in the shadows near the terrace and ensured Miss Hall returned to the ballroom safely before he fled the entertainment altogether.

What had he been thinking? He had almost kissed the chit, which he knew, by the fire that burned in his stomach, the knot of need that clenched within him even now, would have been a kiss to trump all other kisses.

Instead of waiting for his carriage, he ordered it to return home and walked the few blocks to his town house. He needed to work off the feel of Arabella in his arms, her sweet scent of vanilla he could still detect.

He clamped his jaw, stopping several times and looking back at Lord and Lady Delaney's town house, debating if he ought to go back, to drag her from the ballroom and see if the kiss would affect him as much as he feared it would.

Never had he suffered from wanting something he could not have. He liked Arabella. She was personable, amusing, and determined to marry.

Someone else...

Damnit!

What was there not to like about that? She was no threat to him.

He growled. "No threat. She is more of a threat than anyone I've ever met," he mumbled as he strode along. His carriage rolled alongside him, his driver calling out, "Are you certain you wish to walk, my lord?" His driver slowed the horses.

"Actually, no, you may take me home now. I have walked enough." The carriage rolled to a stop, he climbed inside and sighed in relief when they moved forward. Tomorrow night was the Duke and Duchess Renford's ball, and the following evening was his own, where he could do whatever he wished and enjoy whomever he pleased. Mayhap his last paramour would attend, and he could bed her well, slake the lust out of his body and soul that burned through him for a wallflower.

He shook his head, unable to comprehend that he had almost given way to emotions he had no right to feel. He was not interested in marriage. To be tied to one person for a lifetime seemed a nonsensical thing to do.

He was not cut out to be a husband. He was certainly not fit to be a father.

"I like women too much for that," he reminded himself. But even as he said the words aloud, they rang false. A part of him could imagine only one woman warming his bed, married or not, one pretty face that had caught his interest the moment he saw her in his library.

"Enough, man, get a hold of yourself. Remember who you are," he demanded of himself. He would not give way on that. Up until meeting Miss Hall, his life had been gratifying. She would not interrupt his equilibrium. He would get her married as soon as possible and be rid of her. Look on from afar and be happy that she was content and had all her pure heart desired.

The following evening at the Renford ball, Arabella danced with several gentlemen, Lord Russell twice already, much to Lady Southwell's displeasure, and still Lord Wyndham had not raised a brow or exhibited any type of annoyance. The man was beyond vexing. Lord Russell was quite the partner in doing as they planned. He courted her well, whisked her away to dance whenever the opportunity arose, and certainly looked on the verge of marriage.

What the blazes was wrong with Leo that he would not react?

How could he appear in the darkened gardens as if he wished to devour her and, the following night, be as cold as a fish?

"I do not understand. I was certain that he would dislike us dancing again," she mentioned to Lord Russell, trying to keep her visage relaxed and carefree, even with the vexing concern Lord Wyndham was causing her.

"It could be a front, Miss Hall. Many men, myself included, use it to gain what they want. We will not show our hand too soon, lest we lose the power and control of what is happening around us. It is a ploy, and even though Lord Wyndham seems oblivious, it does not mean he is."

"Hmm, well, he is certainly a good actor if bothered." She pursed her lips in thought. "Mayhap, I was incorrect about him. Maybe he does not like me in that way. Perhaps we are only friends, and my wants and needs make me see things, deluding myself into witnessing what is not there."

"Do not give up just yet, Miss Hall. We have only been playing our games for two balls so far. The Season is young, and there are many more nights we can make his lordship jealous, and Lady Southwell too."

"Well, you are lucky in that respect. Lady Southwell accosted me at supper and questioned my friendship with you. I think she was trying to wager whether your courting was real. I boasted, of course, exaggerated my liking of you and left her displeased. I should think you shall get your way before I do."

Lord Russell chuckled, his teasing grin one of pleasure at this news. "Well, since you did me a great service this evening, and there is more to come, I think there is something you should know."

"What is that?" Arabella met his lordship's eyes, unease settling in her stomach when he looked a little concerned at whatever he was going to say.

"As you know, I am friends with Lord Wyndham, and because up until recently, I was set in my bachelor ways, I was not looking for a wife. Because of this, I was often invited to his entertainments."

Arabella schooled her features, pretending not to know what type of *entertainment* Lord Russell was speaking of, but of course, she did know. And those decadent nights she had hoped ceased while they were under their arrangement...

"That is kind of him," she said, fighting to keep her tone light and unaffected.

"Well, there is one being held tomorrow night. No one out of the select set who attends knows, but I thought it might hinder your plan with Lord Wyndham with other gentlemen if they hear the word of this. He is supposed to be making others jealous of his interest in you, but that interest will be watered down if it's heard he's thrown another of his parties."

Arabella sighed. What a tangled weave of deception she was playing. Here she was dancing with another gentleman she had entered an agreement with to make Lord Wyndham jealous, who, in truth, had never shown an inch of interest in her, not until last night.

Well, he had moments where his eyes had given her hope that he cared more than he was saying, but she was never sure. And he had not kissed her.

"Thank you for telling me of this. I shall ask his lordship and see if it is true."

"Oh, it's true. Do not doubt me on that. The question you should be asking Wyndham is if he will go ahead with it."

Arabella nodded, smiling to cover her disappointment. "I will think about it. After all, he is helping me, but I cannot control his life. Even if I should like these balls to cease, he does not have to do as I say."

She was not his wife, and he had made no promises to her. She had a successful night, more so than any she had ever had before, and she knew it was because both Wyndham and now Lord Russell were showing interest.

Several gentlemen she spoke to were very sweet, kind men, not too high in society to make her feel out of place, considering her past. But none of them sparked her heart to beat fast, none made her skin prickle in awareness.

None of them were Lord Wyndham.

CHAPTER
SIXTEEN

The following evening, Leo lounged on a settee in his downstairs parlor and watched as the seedier, racier side of London society took their enjoyment with each other. His guests danced, drank, and made very merry in shadowed corners, and yet, never in his life had any of it ever seemed more purposeless.

What was he doing with his life? Was this who he really was or wanted to be?

A woman with a black mask danced before him, undulating in a manner that would generally spark his desire. She watched him, her hungry eyes asking for a flick of his head, a grin, the crook of his finger urging her to come his way, but he could not.

She rose no desire in him, not an ounce, and the thought left him pondering what the hell had happened to him in the few weeks since his last private event.

Not happy with his ignoring her seductive wiles, the lady sauntered and danced to him, before sitting at his side. Her hand snaked over his chest, rubbing his flesh through his thin shirt, dipping lower still before he reached out and stopped her.

"Not there," he warned, halting her from petting his cock. Her perfume, a rich, overpowering stench that reminded him of stale lavender, assaulted his senses, and he frowned, looking back within the room.

And that's when he saw her.

Arabella. Watching him, watching the lady at his side pawing at him like he was some novelty.

He wasn't. He knew that to his very core. He was a rogue, a libertine who no longer enjoyed these events in the past few weeks.

He did not move, waiting to see what Arabella would do. She wore a mask like everyone else. Her hair lay loose about her shoulders, which he had not seen on her before. He would love to see her long, dark locks spread out over his pillows as he made her come.

It made her cheekbones look higher than usual, her eyes larger, luminescent...with...*annoyance*.

He swallowed and waited with bated breath to see what she would do. Would she come to him? Would she be irritated, jealous, spiteful, or hurt? He had almost kissed her two nights before.

Hell, he would have ravished her if he had taken that leap, but he had not. And now she was here.

The thoughts of what he could do with her, what they could do together, bombarded his mind, and his cock twitched.

"Oh, yes, that's it, my delicious lord. Get hard for me."

The whispered words from the woman at his side pulled him from his daze over Arabella, and he realized she was still petting him, one finger running along the waist of his breeches.

Only then did Arabella start toward him, her steps sure, her dark, stormy gaze focused solely on him. His body trembled with the thought of her being near and here.

She should not be present, and he should certainly not be wanting her the way he was, but damn it all to hell, she had wiggled under his skin, and he wanted her in every way a man wanted a woman.

Do you want her in marriage, too?

The thought drove some sense into him. No, he did not want marriage, but nor could he imagine her being with anyone else.

What the hell did that all mean?

He rubbed a hand over his jaw, allowing the other woman to pet and rub up against his side, trying to tempt him to fuck her.

He wouldn't, of course. She could do whatever she wished, and nothing would entice him this night but the woman heading his way like a queen ruling over her king.

Arabella stood before him. Her taut, displeased mouth and narrowed eyes settled on the woman at his side. "Leave him," she said, her tone low and tinged with warning.

Leo felt the woman at his side still at the caution and giggle. "Come now, we can share him. There's plenty to go around, and I would know, speaking from past experiences." She chuckled again. "He's quite able to please us both simultaneously."

Leo wasn't sure if he should feel shame or pride at having such a reputation, but at the annoyance on Arabella's visage, the small amount he could see of it, he certainly shouldn't boast such abilities to her.

"I will not ask again." Arabella's tone brooked no argument.

"Leo? Are you going to allow this woman to demand I

leave?" the lady at his side asked, the audacity in her high-pitched voice clear to hear.

"I think it is best." He watched Arabella's features smooth with relief, yet her eyes flickered with annoyance.

The woman at his side huffed her displeasure and left them to find her enjoyment elsewhere.

Leo did not see where. His attention remained on Arabella. Damn, she was so pretty when she was irritated.

"Well, hello," he cooed, trying to reach for her but unable to when she stepped out of his reach. He slumped back onto the settee, wondering why she had to be so hard to get, especially when he wanted her so damn much that he could no longer see sense, not with anything.

"What are you doing?" Arabella crossed her arms, fighting the urge to tap her foot simultaneously. "You know these events will not help my cause or make your courting of me look at all truthful. Need I remind you I have not found a husband...yet." Not that she could ask him to stop living his life just because he chose to help her, but still... He suggested it, after all.

"This event was planned before our arrangement, and I could not disappoint everyone." Leo gestured to the room. "Look at my friends enjoying themselves. Would you take that away from them merely because you did not get what you wanted for one evening?"

Arabella narrowed her eyes, her temper taking hold of her common sense. She stepped toward Leo, leaned over him, and pushed him farther into the seat. She held the settee on either side of his head and went all but nose to nose with the fiend.

"Hosting one of your events and tupping a woman

before everyone is not what you agreed. You may hold your events, but if people see you intimate with anyone here, any pretense we create in society will be stated as false. Unless you do not mean to help me, and you're merely playing with me as you allowed that woman to play with you."

"Were you jealous?" he asked, his lips brushing the side of her mouth, his breath whispering against her skin.

Arabella fought not to close the space between them and take what she so desperately wanted. Even now, her breasts ached for his touch, the warmth between her legs leaving her aching with need.

A need for what she could not say, but a craving she knew Leo certainly would know how to soothe.

"To be jealous would mean I must feel something for you. Mayhap I should ask you if you were trying to make me so, and for what nefarious reason that may be."

His eyes darkened, swirled with hunger, and her heart stopped. Her attention dipped to his lips, so close, beckoning, temping her to jump into a world where pleasure reigned supreme, and nothing else mattered. Not society, marriage, expectations, or anything at all.

She felt the light touch of his hand on her thigh, the only separation of skin being her thin evening gown. "I wasn't trying to make you jealous. I was trying to imagine her as you."

His words sent a shock to her core. Everything that she had thought he would say, those words were not it. She let out a little disbelieving laugh, even though the seriousness of his face did not warrant her reaction. "You lie," she stated, standing up and stepping away, determined to leave.

Before she could get a foot from him, his hands clasped

her about her waist, and he wrenched her down onto his lap, holding her in an immovable grip.

His hand clasped her jaw, tipping her face to meet his. "You want me to explain further, Arabella?" His face was far too close to hers for comfort.

She did not say a word, waiting to see what he would say next. Needing to hear what he had to disclose so she could breathe again.

"I had been sitting here, being petted by a woman I did not want. My thoughts were solely on you, where you were, what you were doing, and how I should not be here, but with you, helping you. I tried to fall into the usual spell of seduction, but it would not work this time. Not this night."

His hand let go of her jaw, and his eyes dipped to her lips. He ran a finger across her bottom lip, his eyes darkening with hunger. "All I could think of was how much I want to taste you. I shouldn't, I know. I do not promise anything to you, and you know that, and yet still, I hunger for a taste of you before you become another's. I do not know if I can live not kissing you just once."

Arabella stared at Leo, unable to recognize the rogue she had met so recently. "If we kiss, it can only happen one time. It does not help either of us to play such games." Guilt pricked within her, knowing she was playing many games that Leo was unaware of.

But then, so was he, even if he said he was not. He played with her, made her want things she could not have, and used truth as his excuse.

"Once will be enough. I'll be satisfied."

Arabella nodded, knowing that for her, once would never be enough.

CHAPTER
SEVENTEEN

A dark, dangerous need rose within Leo, and he fought to control the emotions and demands that were running wild within him. Never had he ever wanted a woman as much as he wanted Arabella right at this moment.

His body burned, craved, and fought to do what it wished with her...

But just when he thought he would gain control of the situation, he lost it most spectacularly.

Arabella clasped his jaw in a punishing grip, tipping his chin up so their gazes met and his mind seized. She was a vixen who knew what she wanted and would take it without regret or shame.

Her eyes blazed with determination, with lust that set his blood on fire. His cock hardened, his stomach knotting with expectation. He could barely swallow or catch his breath. She was magnificent, and his.

All his.

"Just one kiss, Leo," she whispered, her eyes holding his.

He nodded, unable to make such a promise aloud, knowing he would never keep it. One kiss would not be enough. How could it be enough when she was as addictive as the finest wine in Europe?

She moved toward him with achingly slow progress, and he almost expired before her lips brushed his. He closed his eyes, reveling in her soft, plump mouth.

God damn it all to hell, he was done for.

He reached for her, clasped her face, and kissed her.

Hard.

His tongue teased hers, and her soft gasp of surprise and mimicking of his actions spurred his eagerness. He devoured her, kissed and supped, nipped and licked her sweet mouth, taunted and teased them both, and drove himself to madness, where he hoped she would meet him.

Somewhere during the kiss, he'd pulled her close, chest to chest, arms entangled in hair, pulling, clasping, driving the other for more.

Through her gown—which did not leave much to his imagination—the low bodice and fine silk, he could feel every inch of Arabella's womanly curves. Her breasts teased his chest, and he wanted nothing more than to strip her bodice down and take one of her sweet, puckered nipples into his mouth, lave it, taunt and tease her, perhaps even bring her to release with just his tongue.

She pulled his hair, ripping his lips from hers, and he opened his eyes, knowing that the awe, the longing he read in her blue gaze matched his.

She was magnificent.

"I think that is a kiss for the ages," she said, slipping from his lap before he could stop her. He went to reach for her again, but she was too quick for him this time, moving away through his throng of guests and out of reach.

He almost called out her name to stop her, to tell her to come back to finish what they'd started, but he caught himself in time. Leo took a calming breath, rubbing a hand over his face and tracking her movements through his drawing room before she stepped into the foyer and was out of sight.

He slumped back in the settee, his body aflame, his cock rigid, his need beyond enduring.

To have her, you will have to marry her, Leo...

He glanced around the room, wondering if this was what he truly wanted, what made him happy. His childhood had not been good, and he had been determined the moment he gained independence to live life to the fullest without concern or discipline. He'd suffered enough of the latter at the hands of his father. He would not endure it for the rest of his life.

And that had sufficed up until now, up until that kiss.

Damn minx had sent his head into a spin, but he would not act rashly. He would not react and do anything foolish, like propose merely to get her into his bed.

He could have any woman here this night. His lips curled at the thought of sleeping with anyone but Arabella.

She wants a love match, Leo...

And that he could never give her, no matter how much she spiked his desire. He would continue to help her, guide her, and remember their one kiss with pleasure.

A kiss to last all time.

A lifetime.

Arabella ran to her room when she returned to Lord and Lady Lupton-Gage's home and shut and locked her door. She ripped her gown from her body, moving toward the chamber she used for washing, and splashed cold water over her face.

It went in some way to cool her overheated flesh.

A temperature that was scalding hot after her kiss with Leo.

The memory of his tongue teasing hers, his hot, whisky-fueled breath, his soft lips, and his wicked mouth.

Oh, dear heavens... She placed a hand on her brow, certain it was still scalding hot, even after the time had passed since she had left his town house.

She had gone there to confront him, to demand he hold up their bargain, only to succumb to his charms. The moment she slumped onto his lap, she knew she would not leave without sampling a little of Leo's wickedness.

She bit her lip, looking at herself in the looking glass, trying to recognize the young woman she was, who had been in this room earlier that night.

But she was gone. Perhaps forever.

In her place stood a young woman touched by desire. A woman who had kissed a man and kissed him well. A woman who had fallen into the clutches of a rake and never wished to be let go again.

Her eyes stared back at her, large and full of questions, and knowledge, too.

That kiss...

She took a deep, calming breath and returned to her bedroom, removing her shift and replacing it with a night dress. Her maid would wonder at her gowns strewn about her room in the morning, but she would never tell what she had been up to, what she had experienced.

How wonderful all of it had been.

Was this why Evie and even Reign looked at their husbands with a hidden, secretive glance that appeared wicked and knowing? Did they experience such kisses with their husbands?

How lucky they both were if that were true.

Arabella lay on her bed for several minutes, reliving the kiss, going over every delicious memory she had. The kiss would only happen once, a fleeting, scandalous action that she would not experience again.

The thought of marrying another man, having him kiss her in that way, seemed awfully wrong. At present, she could not think of one gentleman courting her who would make her feel the way Leo had this evening.

Still, her heart beat fast, her skin prickled, her stomach knotted with need.

Need of him... But what did that mean?

She punched the bed with her fists, hating the fact that young women such as herself were kept in the dark when it came to men and what they expected of their wives once married.

Why, however, was a mystery. Who would not wish to know that marriage to a man would include such kisses, tender touches, and words?

But there was more to marriage than kisses. What, she could not say, and she really ought to ask Reign of it before she accepted any gentleman. She disliked being ignorant and did not wish to make a fool of herself on her wedding night.

She reached down, touching her body, imagining Leo feeling her instead. This evening, shamefully, she had wanted him to touch her, to move his hand from her face and clasp her aching breasts.

She wanted him to lay her down on the settee they had sat on and be the rake he was so famous for. Try to seduce her to his every desire and whim.

When he kissed her, she doubted she would have said no, that she would have pushed him away and refused his suit.

Something hungry and full of longing told her she would have opened her arms to his every wish, given him what he wanted, and gladly so.

Give him what she wanted too.

CHAPTER
EIGHTEEN

L eo did not attend any balls or parties for the next several days, knowing it would not be safe to do so. Not for Miss Arabella Hall, in any case.

Even now, three days after he'd had her on his lap, kissing the woman who haunted him in his dreams, he wanted her still. Wanted to pull her into a darkened room, or moonlit garden, and see what other enjoyable evenings they could have together.

But there was no getting out of the yearly ball held by his good, if not infamous, friend Lord Marshall at Vauxhall.

The invitations had gone out weeks ago, and most of the *ton*, including those from the *beau monde* and *demi-monde*, would be there, a mixture of classes all resolved to have a night of revelry and amusement, if not a little scandal.

Not that Miss Arabella Hall would be in attendance. Debutantes were not invited to attend, and nor should they be since Lord Marshall's ball was not for the faint of heart or pure mind, which all debutantes *should* be.

Leo almost scoffed at the idea of Arabella being pure of mind after the kiss they shared.

He closed his eyes and leaned back into the squabs of his carriage as it made its way through London toward Vauxhall. He could almost smell her sweet vanilla, an intoxicating fragrance he had not been able to remove from his memory. The feel of her on his lap, all womanly curves, the little mews of enjoyment as their tongues danced, as their lips meshed, devoured.

Leo adjusted his seat, moving his cock to sit better against his falls. What was it about this chit that drove him to distraction? He had never been chaste and had always loved to live without rules and boundaries, especially once he had been old enough to take rooms at the Albany. But Arabella tempted him to throw over his lifestyle and enjoy a different and new type with her.

He shook his head and ran a hand over his jaw. He would not, of course. Stepping toward marriage meant giving up what he fought so hard to achieve.

Independence, freedom, and, above all, happiness.

He arrived at Vauxhall by the time the ball was well engaged, with hundreds of guests already enjoying their night of revelry. Lord Marshall had outdone himself, hiring circus performers, dancers, and an opera singer who sparked Leo's interest wildly when she threw him a naughty wink.

A notion to look into later tonight, once he'd partaken in several beverages.

All thoughts of the opera singer ripped from his mind as the crowd before him parted, and he spied Lord and Lady Lupton-Gage talking with Miss Hall and several other known acquaintances.

He shut his mouth with a snap, biting down on the

expletive he wanted to curse aloud, and bit his tongue. What the hell were they doing here? What were they thinking, bringing a debutante to such a ball?

This was not appropriate.

Arabella laughed at something Lord Russell said, her attention moving about the park and those attending, but her attention stopped when she spotted him.

Like a bolt of lightning, his body felt the full force of her interest. He noted everything about her with aching accuracy, the little flyaway curls that brushed her cheek. Her large, intelligent gaze that felt as though she read him like a book left him vulnerable and open, unable to hide anything from her. Her lush, plump lips opened in a silent gasp.

Dear God in heaven, she was his walking, breathing, tempting hell.

Without thinking, he grabbed the first woman who stepped past him and swept her into a dance. The lady, one whom he had never seen before in his life, laughed and threw herself into the impromptu dance with glee, helping him have the time to gather his wits.

"Oh, my lord, you are joyful this evening. I'm so pleased to dance with you."

Leo frowned, glanced down at the woman, and wondered if he knew her and how. *Please do not let it be a woman whom I've had sexual interactions with and cannot remember...*

"Have we met?" he asked, forcing his attention on the woman in his arms and not Arabella, whom he could see out of his peripheral vision was talking to a gentleman who had joined their group.

"No, but your reputation precedes you. I'm happy to get to know you better this evening, if that is your wish."

Ah, so he was dancing with a cyprian, which would do

him well, for now. "I'm afraid I'm only here to enjoy the dancing and company, nothing else."

"A pity," she said, pouting up at him. "I would have made your night more fun than it ultimately will be."

Leo chuckled and did not mention that it would not be her that made his night more enjoyable, but rather another pretty, intoxicating, frustrating beauty whom he was supposed to be helping find a husband. Not seduce as his mind and soul seemed to have shifted to wanting instead these past days.

He would need to avoid her, not tempt himself more than he already was.

Arabella danced with Lord Russell and threw herself into the country dance. As the dance progressed, she changed multiple partners, discussing short, inconsequential topics before moving on to her next.

But the moment her fingers entwined with large, strong hands that encased hers with a tenderness that left her breathless, she knew she had stepped into the arms of Lord Wyndham, and all other partners dissipated in her memory.

"What are you doing here?" he asked her, his voice harsher than she'd expected.

She looked up at him as they walked the few steps forward in the dance. "I came with Lord and Lady Lupton-Gage. I have never been to Vauxhall before, and they were invited. There is nothing wrong with me being here." If Arabella's tone was frostier than usual, it was Lord Wyndham's fault. Why would he chastise her, especially after their shared kiss?

A kiss that still haunted her every waking moment of her life.

"This ball is but an outdoor version of my own. Lord Lupton-Gage should not have brought you here."

Arabella flinched at his annoyance. Did he not want her here at all? Was he mad that they had kissed? Did he think she was following him about now that they had shared such an intimacy?

"Do not make yourself unwell with worry regarding me, my lord. I'm quite capable of keeping out of your way so you may enjoy your night. I came with my family, nothing more than that. I did not know you would be here, if it interests you."

His lordship's growl of annoyance furthered her hurt and confusion. What was wrong with him this evening?

"You should ask to leave before you are privy to situations that are not appropriate."

"Well, you may discuss such notions with Lord Lupton-Gage, for I certainly will not be bringing up the subject." Arabella wrenched out of his hold and walked from the outdoor ballroom, leaving Lord Wyndham alone and without a partner.

She heard his hurried footsteps behind her, and she merely walked faster, moving through guests as quickly as she could to avoid him. Her chest hurt with the memory of his words, coldness, and disapproval.

She should never have kissed him. She had probably muddled up her chances of winning him.

How would she spend time with Lord Wyndham if he no longer helped her? If they were no longer friends.

Where she was walking, she did not know. All she knew was that she needed to flee Leo, calm her emotions, and bite back the tears that threatened her.

How dare he upset her so? Tell her off like a child not old enough to know right from wrong, good from bad. Well, she certainly knew right at this moment that Lord Wyndham was being an ass, and she did not wish to speak to him at all.

"Arabella, stop." His words were close enough that she ought to heed his warning, but she did not.

Instead, she increased her pace and hoped he would give up. Best that he did before his chastisement was returned twofold, and by her. The marquess and future duke needed a set down, and she was more than willing to give him one if he persisted in chasing her through the throng of Vauxhall guests.

CHAPTER
NINETEEN

Leo wrenched Arabella to a halt behind a row of supper boxes. Behind the stone structure, the music and voices quieted, allowing them peace and time to speak. Not that Arabella looked particularly interested in talking to him. She looked more inclined to scold him all the way back to London.

She pulled her arm free of his hold, and he cringed, hating having manhandled her in that way.

He took a step back and checked himself mentally, not liking the primitive, obsessive thoughts he had when he was around her. Such reflections were not helpful, not to either of them.

"I have every right to be at this ball, which we were invited to, just as you were. I know," she said, cutting him off when he went to argue that point, "that my being here may make your plans to rut your way through every willing woman here at Vauxhall difficult, or at least uncomfortable due to our agreement. You may feel ill at ease, but let me be clear, my lord. You do not get to tell me, a man I'm not engaged or married to, where I can and cannot visit. You do not own me, and even if I were your wife and you tried to stop me from attending an event, you would know if I disapproved."

Leo crossed his arms, forcing himself to keep his hands to himself, even though he wanted to wrench her into his arms and kiss her pursed, displeased mouth, sending them both tumbling toward a more pleasant interlude.

"You are right, of course," he found himself saying, but still, it was not right that she was indeed here. "But Vaux-hall is no place for innocent women such as yourself. And it would certainly help if you had not fled as you did. What if I had not caught up with you? What if you unthinkingly fled into the gardens and were attacked? Unfortunately, you would not be the first to befall such a fate."

Arabella swallowed and glanced at the gardens before raising her chin defiantly. "I would not have fled had you not chastised me like a child."

"I know you're not a child." He knew that fact, to his very detriment. This evening, Arabella wore a gown of golden silk stitched with a silver decorative design about her bodice and puffy sleeves. She was so utterly beautiful that each time he looked at her, he forgot his reasons as to why he would not court the woman to marry.

"I would have thought after our kiss that fact would have been clearer to you, my lord." Her words sent a bolt of desire, memory, and need to course through him. He ground his teeth, forcing himself not to move or touch her. "That was a mistake. We're friends, and I agreed to help you. The kiss was uncalled for."

She threw him a look that dripped with sarcasm. "So you do not wish to kiss me again? I hold no interest in you besides finding me a good, meek, biddable husband."

"Is that not what we agreed? Although I cannot remember you asking for a biddable husband."

She shrugged, slumping against the stone wall of the supper box. "I added that requirement just now. After our conversation, I will not have a husband who orders me about and lords it over me."

Shame washed through him that he had been the reason for her words. He did not want to lord over anyone, and certainly did not want to throw orders about and expect to be obeyed by a woman who wasn't his.

The image of his father chastising him, and his mother for letting her small son enjoy a day playing out in the gardens at their country estate, floated through his memory. He had ended the day with a good, scalded bottom, and his mother a bruised eye.

"I never wished to make you feel that way, Miss Hall. Forgive me if I managed to do so." Leo turned to leave, not liking that a woman was made to feel as he had so often felt himself at the hands of his father.

Worthless.

"Wait," Arabella called, her hand clasping Leo's and pulling him to a stop. "We need to speak."

Leo turned, and the pain in his eyes sent her heart crumbling. Whatever had she said to have affected him so much? She had scolded him a little for his highhandedness, but he looked genuinely distraught.

"I do not wish to keep you from enjoying your night. Lord Russell is here, and I'm certain he's probably looking to dance with you again."

Arabella wanted to wave away his suggestion she allow Lord Russell to court her. They were playing their games to get what they wanted, not that Leo was aware of such schemes. Even so, she did not want to speak to him about that.

"I do not want to talk of Lord Russell. I want to discuss us and ensure you will still help me find a husband, even if you are disappointed I'm here this evening."

"Of course, you still have my assistance. I gave you my word. I will not break it."

Arabella watched him, trying to discern if he was being honest. "Even after our kiss? That has not changed your opinion of me? I know it was not very ladylike what I allowed us to do."

He stepped close, his attention dipping to her lips, and heat pooled at her core. Her legs shook. Need thrumming through her that would not relent, nor did she wish it to. She wanted to stoke those flames, add fuel to the fire between them, and tempt his lordship to take a chance outside his everyday behavior.

Take a chance on me.

"A kiss never hurt anyone and you're old enough to experience your first. I'm glad it was with me and not some shoddy fellow who did not know what he was doing."

She bit back a grin, glad the teasing, flirtatious Lord Wyndham was back. "I have wondered what Lord Russell's kisses would be like and if they would differ from yours. Do you think he knows how to kiss?" she asked, not the least interested in such a question but needing to spark, to prod Lord Wyndham into realizing that she could not wait forever for him to decide about her or marriage.

Not that she knew if he were at all thinking along such lines, but she had to try. Living the rest of her life wondering what if would drive her insane.

"I'm sure he knows what to do," his lordship said, his voice low with disinterest.

"Do you think he'll like kissing me? Did you enjoy kissing me, or did I make a terrible mess of it all?" Arabella stared at him with a boldness she did not feel. Her innards tumbled and clenched with nerves, but she held her stance and waited for him to reply.

"I cannot answer your first question, but as for your second, I know I enjoyed our kiss very much. You're quick to learn the art of seduction."

"Is that what it is? A kiss, I mean," she asked. "A seduction?"

A muscle worked in his jaw, and he nodded. "Yes, that's exactly what a kiss is. Of course."

Arabella bit her lip, the urge to experience another one overriding her self-control. "I think I shall go and find Lord Russell and see if I can steal him away from the ball. Mayhap, with a little privacy, I may be able to test what I desperately want to know."

She took a step around him, and his arms clasped about her waist, pulling her up hard against his chest. Arabella stilled, but did not fight his hold. The thumping of his heart, his hard, corded muscles pressed against her back, left her legs weak, and she could not have wrenched from him if she had tried.

"Was there something else you wished to say, my lord?"

His lips brushed the underside of her ear, working his way down her neck before she felt the ticklish slide of his tongue on her shoulder blade. "There is more to desire, to need, than a kiss. Lord Russell needs to spark every wanton and secretive desire you hold." His hand slipped up her waist and, with perfect, achingly delicious ability, kneaded one of her breasts. His thumb circled where her nipple poked through her silk gown before he rolled it between two of his fingers.

Arabella moaned and did not care how the sound made her appear. Wetness pooled between her legs, and she squeezed them tight, needing to give herself a little relief, but from what, she frustratingly did not know.

TWENTY

S he covered his hand with hers, pressing him harder against her breast. She felt him still, his manhood against the apex of her bottom.

"Arabella." Her name whispered with such pain and wanting against her ear, sent a shiver of desire down her spine that would not be repressed.

She turned, pushed against his shoulders, and walked him backward until he came up hard against the supper box wall himself. "What, my lord?" she asked boldly. "You cannot expect to touch me so and not have me respond."

He did not say a word, merely watched her, waiting for her to make the next move. His eyes swirled, darkened with hunger, and gave her the boldness she would have otherwise lacked.

Arabella already knew what she would do next, but whether he would allow it would be another matter entirely. She lay her hand against his chest, feeling his magnificent muscles beneath her palms. Sandalwood and desire teased her senses and made her braver than usual.

She lowered her hand, running one finger along the

edge of his silk breeches. She met his gaze, his eyes wild and wide, and she understood his concern, his hunger, for it was hers too, and she would do what she wanted. Even if only this night.

She dipped her hand lower still, sliding it over his rigid manhood and feeling him through his silk breeches. A pained expression crossed his features, and he lay his head against the wall, closing his eyes as she learned every nuance of his manhood.

He was thick, long, bigger than she had thought men ought to be, considering a man's member entered a woman's body. Would he even fit? Would she enjoy such a joining?

The moisture, the tingling warmth between her legs, told her she would, but still, it was a foreign, odd thing to imagine, even if she wanted to.

"You must stop, Arabella," he groaned, his words going against what his body was seeking as he pushed into her hold, undulating against her palm.

"You want me to stop?" The more she touched him, the more confident she became in her learning of him. She watched with fascination as he sucked in a startled breath, his tongue dampening his lips when she tightened her hold, clasping him through his breeches and stroking him.

"No," he admitted at length, his eyes heavy with desire, his lips twisted into a teasing grin. "But you should before you make me spend in my breeches, and I'll have to leave you here."

Arabella sighed, not wanting to let him go. Although she had never been so brazen before, the idea that Leo allowed her to touch him, tease him, stroke him toward spending in his breeches, whatever that meant, gave her more gumption and nerve than she had ever had before.

"What does spend mean?" She had to know, wanted to learn all there was between a man and a woman.

He clasped her face in his hands and kissed her so softly, so sweetly that Arabella was sure she was floating for a heartbeat or two. This could not be real. He could not be so caring, not if he felt nothing toward her except the desire to see her happily married to someone else.

There had to be more between them, and she was determined to find out how much.

S *he's not yours, Leo.*
    The warning clambered through his mind as he kissed her and fell under her spell. For a few moments more, he reveled in her response to him, her lips soft and supple, kissing him back with a need, an urgency he had started to feel himself.

Not that he wanted to delve into what that urgency was. Not right now, and perhaps never if Arabella married someone else.

He reluctantly pulled back, watched as she blinked, and realized where and what they were doing. At least, that was what he hoped she was doing. For him, he certainly was not in his right mind. In fact, he had started to think he'd bloody well lost it completely.

"You should return to Lord and Lady Lupton-Gage," he warned, on the precipice of losing his ability to keep from touching her, teasing her as much as she teased him.

She did not heed his warning. Instead, the vixen leaned against him, closing the space that separated them, and wrapped her arms around his neck. "I do not want to return just yet, not when you're teaching me so much more, helping me in my endeavors to win a husband." She flicked her chin toward the sound of the music. "I know how to dance, talk, and partake in society as I should, but you, Lord Wyndham, can teach me the other side of marriage and what it entails, and I'm now fascinated by it."

Dear Lord in heaven, he had not meant to tempt her so much that she now desired him in the art of seduction. Should he step toward that slippery pitch, there would be no climbing back up.

"Do not tempt me, Miss Hall. I'm not a man to be trifled with, certainly not petted and stroked and then left with no relief. I'm allowing you to leave before I ask more of you than you're willing to give."

"And what if I wish to give it all to you?" Her hand slipped over his crotch a second time, and he gasped, grabbing her wrist to still her pawing.

"I'll not marry you," he warned, hoping she would heed his last caution.

"I have not asked you to." She reached for his other hand, placing it on her breast. "I want you to touch me. I want to feel as you do."

Leo inwardly quivered, fighting for self-control that would not rise to the occasion. Only his cock was growing in this circumstance, and that was not helpful at all.

"Please, Leo."

Her words broke the last of his control, and he clasped her hand and dragged her farther into the darkened Vauxhall gardens. For several steps, he moved them away from the threat of discovery and into a small hedge that housed a little stone seat nestled within it.

She did not protest, merely followed him, and the moment they were out of sight of the supper boxes, he wrenched her into his arms and kissed her as he'd wanted to kiss her from the moment he'd seen her this evening.

Their tongues fought and danced for supremacy, but he would win this war this night. She wanted to feel as he did. Well, she would feel everything, and he would not relent until she shattered in his arms.

He hoisted up her gown, enjoying the feel of her soft thigh as he worked his hand toward her mons. He feathered touches across her sensitive flesh and smiled when she gasped at his boldness.

"Put one leg up on the seat. I'm going to pet you as you pet me."

She did as he said, watching him, her eyes bright and glistening with need, with expectation.

He touched her wet, sensitive flesh, sliding his finger gently over her engorged nubbin. Oh yes, she was wet and ready for him; her touching of him had made her wanton.

She bit her lip as he stroked her, teased her notch before dipping the tip of his finger into her hot, tight heat.

"Leo," she gasped, undulating against his hand, pushing him farther into her.

"You like that?" he breathed against her lips, dipping his tongue out to wet her lips. "Do you want me to do more? How far are you willing to go, Arabella?"

"As far as you're willing to take me." She kissed him hard before he wrenched free and eased her down to sit on the stone bench.

"Pool your dress at your waist. I'm going to fuck you with my mouth."

"Pardon?" she gasped, the first slight tremor in her words giving him pause. "You're going to do what?"

He knelt, helping her with her gown. The sight of her, open and exposed before him, her wet cunny glistening in the moonlit night, made his mouth water. "I'm going to give you so much satisfaction that you'll not regret this night."

"I would never regret anything." She leaned back, opening her legs farther.

Leo swallowed, never wanting to taste a woman as bad as he wanted to taste her. "I won't take your maidenhead, but you will experience such bliss, just as I promised."

She nodded and waited, and he did not allow her to defer long. He leaned forward, set her legs atop his shoulders, and licked along the edge of her quim.

Their moans mingled as he tasted her for the first time, sweet and as delicious as he feared she would be, a temptress that would never be his except this one night.

He would make sure it was one she always remembered.

TWENTY-ONE

Arabella did not know what came over her, allowing such liberties, nor could she stop what her body craved to experience with Leo. She wanted him, with a bottomless, gut-wrenching appetite that would not diminish, and nothing and no one would stop her from getting what she wanted.

Even if it were only for one night, they slipped into this pretend life that she desperately wanted to come true.

His mouth, his tongue, which she had never imagined could be used as such an erotic tool, laved her cunny and teased a place upon her that wept for more.

She bit her lip, unable to hold back the moan that escaped when he dipped one finger into her achingly wet core.

"Leo," she gasped, undulating against his face, taking from him what he so freely gave. The sweet delectation of his every stroke, his soft suckling that almost spiraled her off the bench, was beyond reason or sense.

What was he doing to her?

He worked her carefully, gently, built up the fire that

simmered in her blood until she burned for release, for him to give her everything her mind could conjure.

Her fingers tangled in his hair, holding him against her. He did not relent, continued to assault, to tease, to be utterly wicked with his mouth, and then she felt it. The rippling, unequivocal, delightful convulsions started between her legs and spread to every part of her body. Arabella moaned his name, a senseless tirade of thanks and more, and did not stop.

He did not. He kissed her and drew out every last tremor of release that he could.

He rocked back on his heels, his eyes heavy with desire, and slipped her gown back over her legs. Arabella could not form words and could not catch her breath.

Never had she ever experienced such pleasure. Was this what occurred every time a husband and wife were alone? And they had not even had sexual relations, so was that even better than this?

She could not imagine anything being more pleasing.

He licked his lips and used his thumb to wipe the corner of his mouth, his wicked grin one of pride and accomplishment. "You sound like you enjoyed our little interlude."

He stood and reached out a hand. Arabella took it and ignored the fact her fingers shook. "I do not know what just happened, but I understand that I have never experienced anything so wonderful."

He leaned down and kissed her lips softly, lingering there when she reached to keep him close. She could taste herself on him, and that in itself left her wanting more. "I'll escort you back to the ball. You'll be missed if we do not return soon."

They started to head back, but Arabella pulled him to a stop. "When will I see you again?"

"The Finchs' ball tomorrow evening as agreed. We still have to find you a husband, do we not?"

His eyes held hers, and she wondered if he was stating what they had agreed or asking her if she still wanted a husband. At this stage, she certainly wanted one, so long as it was Leo, and he made love to her as wickedly as he had tonight.

"Of course," she said, wanting to ensure she saw him again.

"Well then, tomorrow night, Miss Hall." He returned her to Lord and Lady Lupton-Gage and made small talk with his lordship for several minutes before excusing himself and disappearing into the crowd of guests.

As much as she tried to find him during the course of the ball, she did not spy him anywhere, and she could only assume that he left Vauxhall after departing their company.

At least, that was what she hoped. Another dark, unnerving thought would not relent that he had found one of the many whores here this evening and bought their services since he had not seen the pleasure that she had in the gardens.

Arabella frowned. Maybe she should have asked him what she could do for him. Indeed, if a woman could find such pleasure without sex, a man could also...

A notion she would ask his lordship tomorrow night and see what he could inform her on the matter.

The following evening, Leo arrived at Lord and Lady Finch's ball, determined to end the agreement between Arabella and himself. After what he had done to her last night, the absurdness had to stop.

He could not seduce her in such a way and think that

was appropriate. Even if she did enjoy every sinful slide of his tongue against her carvel's ring, he could not do it again. And at this point, the only way he could keep from wanting her was to avoid her.

He spied her dancing with Lord Russell, and they were smiling at each other in a way that set the hairs on the back of his neck to stand on end. Was this the gentleman she wished to marry?

Leo studied the earl. He was handsome, rich, and connected, of course, and more than capable of satisfying a woman; his entertainment reputation had proven that, but was he good enough for Arabella?

He narrowed his eyes. No, he unequivocally was not.

Lord Russell may start in his marriage as a faithful husband, but it would not be long before he reverted to his ways. Even from afar, Leo did not want to see Arabella lose hope and faith in the man she loved.

He liked her too much to see such a tragedy occur to her. She was already on the outer edges of society due to her upbringing. He would not allow her to marry a man who would also give the *ton* an excuse to ridicule and pity her.

Nor could he keep from her, keep from seducing her, if he knew she was unhappy...

The dance ended, and before Leo knew what he was about, he reached for Arabella's hand and pulled her into his arms for the next. The notes of a waltz started.

Perfect, just the type of dance he required to speak to her, and being so public with their exchange, he would not be tempted to devour her on the ballroom floor.

Vanilla floated through the air, making him remember last evening in full force. His cock hardened, his blood pumped fast in his veins. Damn, he needed to get a hold of himself before everyone present knew how much Miss Arabella Hall affected him.

"Lord Wyndham, I did not know you had arrived," she said, her voice unaffected, her eyes barely meeting his as she concentrated on something over his shoulder.

He turned to see what it was, and annoyance thrummed through him that it was Lord Russell, standing at the side of the ballroom floor, his small smile just for Arabella making Leo's palm itch to slap the man back into his senses.

Russell was not for her.

"I have changed my mind regarding Lord Russell. He's a rogue, perhaps a worse one than I am, and would not make a suitable husband. I'm sure he will tire of you before the first month of marriage. You must look elsewhere. I thought Lord St. Rolle may suffice."

Arabella stilled in his arms and finally met his gaze. Determination and annoyance simmered in her blue eyes, not what he had expected to see. "Well, I think he will do perfectly well. At least he did not disappear last evening as someone else in my presence did."

Leo watched her and noted the displeased line of her mouth. "Where do you think I went to last night, Miss Hall?" he asked, trying to keep their interaction the least intimate as possible, but knowing he was going to fail miserably.

"Much like everyone else, I assumed you bedded some cyprian at the ball. You were in quite a state, and I can only assume you were as affected as I was from our interaction, and since I did not help you gain your pleasure, I believe you would have sought it elsewhere."

If he had expected Arabella to say anything, what she declared was not it. He shut his mouth with a snap and fought not to remember how she tasted, her little mewls of pleasure, her undulating against his mouth as he kissed her to release.

God damn it all to hell, he wanted her.

"I did not fuck anyone," he whispered, more harshly than he intended. But with his cock raging in his breeches, he was less than pleased. "Would you prefer to know that I went home immediately after I left you, locked my bedroom door, stroked my cock so hard, pulled my prick with such force, imagining that I was fucking you instead? That I imagined I bent you over that stone bench I had you on, hoisted your skirts against your sweet ass, and impaled you with my cock, filling you, stroking your wet heat until we both collapsed in debauchery. Is that what you want to hear?"

At some point during his verbal tirade, they had stopped dancing. Arabella stared at him, her eyes wide, but not with fear or shock, but longing.

Blast it. That was not what he wanted her to feel.

She fled the dance floor, and he followed, ignoring the interested glances their departure caused. All he knew was he had to talk sense into her. Make her believe and understand he was too much for her, too broken and set in his ways.

Too much a rake to ever mend his ways, even for her.

TWENTY-TWO

Arabella walked away from Lord Wyndham, needing to clear her mind of the inappropriate yet tempting images he had placed within her head. How could she continue to dance, pretend to be interested in anyone else when the man, the very one she wanted above all others, taunted her with his words?

Had he really done those things to himself? Had she put him into a position where he had to relieve his pent-up frustrations with his hand?

She started up the stairs, ignoring Lord Wyndham's presence behind her, even at a respectable distance. But instead of heading toward the retiring room, she diverted in the opposite direction. A door loomed at her left, and she opened it, not knowing where she was going or for how long. But before she could close the door to what turned out to be a small linen closet, Lord Wyndham joined her, only then shutting them inside.

Alone.

"You should not have followed me. Someone may have seen."

"No one saw," he growled, the light from under the door their only source. He moved toward her, pushing her farther into the space until her back came up against a cupboard full of linens.

"What do you think you're doing, my lord? We're not courting, and you do not want to marry, so you should not be here."

His eyes flickered with an emotion, and she swallowed down the nerves. She had never seen him so determined, and something about his deep, calm voice put her on edge.

"I'm being selfish. I know you're looking elsewhere. Perhaps you have even decided on Lord Russell, but after having tasted you, I cannot deny myself more of you before you're no longer mine to have."

Arabella could barely believe what he was saying. "I will not be your plaything, Leo. No matter how much we may have enjoyed our little tryst the other evening, that does not mean it can happen again."

A muscle worked in his jaw, and his penetrating gaze would not relent. "I want you to shatter in my arms again. I do not think I can survive another night without hearing your raspy breaths against my ear as you come."

She shivered, clasped the cupboard behind her, and let out a little yelp when he closed the space between them and kissed her.

Kissed her so soundly, with deep, determined strokes, that she lost all coherent thought. Somewhere, somehow, Arabella lost control of the situation and kissed him back, clung to him, undulated against him, and strove to feel that delicious release he had given her the night before.

His hands clasped her bottom, pulling her against his engorged manhood. Arabella wrapped one leg about his hip, undulating, teasing her excited flesh. She kissed him, long and deep, and moaned when the tingling, thrumming sensations started to ache between her legs.

"Arabella," Leo gasped, both lost in their exchange. Even with them both fully clothed, the friction, the slide, and the force of their actions built a fire within her that teased and promised a release similar to what he had given her before. "I'm going to come," he admitted.

She nodded, gripping his nape as the trembling started to echo from between her legs and spiral out into every ounce of her body.

"Leo," she gasped as pleasure tore through her, tremor after tremor, delicious ache after ache, as she found her release for a second time in his arms.

"Oh, Arabella." Leo pressed harder against her groin, grinding her with a savageness that only heightened her release. She held on to him, fought for purchase, and knew she would never gain it. Not when she was in his arms. "I'm coming too," he growled.

They ground against each other for several heartbeats, wringing every last piece of the release. Their breathing ragged, Leo kissed her softly before stepping out of her hold and standing a foot from her.

Arabella swallowed and fought to regain her composure. Her heart thumped loudly in her ears, and she was certain he could hear what he did to her, how much he affected her.

She could not look away from him, drank in his every wicked feature. He appeared so handsome in his dark superfine coat and neatly tied cravat. He looked as collected and aristocratic as ever, even after what they had partaken in.

He watched her, his stormy, hooded gaze oozing with

need still. "You must know how much I want to fuck you right now."

"We should not cross that line, my lord," she warned, clasping the cupboard behind her, unsure what he would do. What she would do should he reach for her again.

Something told her that she would relent, give him what he wanted, what they both wanted.

"No, we should not." He ran a hand through his hair, turned on his heel, and left, slamming the door behind him.

Arabella let out a relieved breath, having never felt so overwhelmed, so out of control when she was around a man. He drew from her a side that was untamed and wanton. Two things that would surely lead to ruin with no chance of redemption, not even if it was in his arms.

Leo slumped onto the squabs of his carriage, but if he thought to have a moment's peace, he was mistaken. A woman barreled in after him, and before he could tell her to leave, the door closed, and the carriage lurched forward.

"What are you doing? You cannot be in my carriage, Arabella."

She shrugged one of her lovely shoulders, her collarbone that he had run his tongue along at Vauxhall, tempting him beyond endurance. The urge to go to her, to pull her into his arms and have a taste of her again, almost overrode his senses.

"Our conversation in the closet was not over, so I followed you. I will return to the ball after I get what I want."

Dread settled in his gut, and he took a deep breath. "Get what you want. What do you mean?" he asked. He thought about ordering his driver to return to Lord and Lady Finch's town house and be free of this torment, but something stopped him.

He fisted his hands when she moved to sit beside him, and then, taking the breath out of his lungs, she straddled him. He dared not touch her for fear of where that would end.

She tipped his face up to look at her. In the shadowed carriage, her eyes burned with determination, and Leo knew that his strength of character was about to be tested.

She pressed against his already engorged cock, and he hissed out a breath, forcing himself not to touch her. "I want you, Leo. I want you to do those things to me you mentioned in your thoughts. I want what you teased me with before I'm no longer yours to have."

The idea that she would be anyone else's broke what little restraint he had left. He whipped her around to lay upon the seat so fast she let out a squeal of alarm that turned into a guttural chuckle when he kissed her.

Hard.

They came together with a force unknown to him. Never had he been seized with the need to own, to dominate, to take what was offered freely to him, to put his mark on her.

His.

Mine.

Now and forever...

She helped him in his endeavors, shuffling up her dress, and he ripped his falls open. His cock sprang into his hand, and he teased them both, rubbing it against her wet, aching flesh before he could wait not a moment longer.

She wrapped her legs around his waist, and he took her, forgoing niceties. Later, he would regret such passion, but at the moment, when she gasped his name, begged him to take her, make her his, he could not control the wildness that overtook his soul.

He thrust into her, taking her, his cock rigid and pushing her toward release. He would not spend until she had shattered in his arms. Again and again, they rocked together and found a rhythm that suited them both, but still, it was not enough.

He wanted more.

So. Much. More.

"Leo," she gasped, the first tremors of her release clamping around his cock with such force that his head spun.

"Come for me, Arabella. Come hard," he commanded, wanting her to shatter, to lose control, to break free of the restraints that so many women lived within in this life.

Her fingers clutched at his back, her nails marking his skin through his superfine coat, and he came the instant he heard his name on her lips, a cry, a plea, to take her, give her his all.

He would not disappoint. He rode their wave of pleasure, spiraling with Arabella until only the two of them existed in the world in which they lived.

For this night, at least.

CHAPTER
TWENTY-THREE

The following morning, Arabella woke, bathed, and dressed in a soft, sky-blue muslin morning gown. She broke her fast with Lord and Lady Lupton-Gage and was happy to hear that Evie, now Duchess Ruthven, would be in town the following week.

She shifted her seat, noting yet again the soreness that accompanied her today. A blush burned on her cheeks, remembering what she had done in the carriage with Lord Wyndham. How he had taken her with a fierce appetite that, even now, she longed for again, if he were willing.

She sipped her tea and listened to the idle morning chatter before what Lady Lupton-Gage said pulled her from her musings.

"What do you think, Arabella?"

"What do I think?" she asked, having no idea what the conversation was about and hating that she hadn't been paying much attention.

"About the announcement in the paper this morning that Lord Wyndham is now the Duke Carnavon. His father passed last night."

"He passed away?" Her cup clattered down on its plate, and she stared at Reign, unable to comprehend that what she was saying was true. Leo was a duke? Had he lost his only remaining parent? How sad he must be.

"Yes, from an apoplexy of the heart, they're saying." Reign clasped her chest as if hers, too, was seizing. "How sad for Lord Wyndham...I mean His Grace. I suppose that will mean we will no longer see him in society."

Arabella nodded, supposing that would be right. He would go into mourning for a year at least, as it was frowned upon to entertain or attend social events during that time.

Despair swamped her that he would no longer be able to help her find a husband, even though the only husband she wanted was him. But nor would he be present to see her flirt and flutter her eyelashes toward Lord Russell to make him jealous.

Arabella pushed the selfish thoughts aside, hating that she was shallow enough to think of herself during this difficult time for Leo.

"May I be excused? I may go for a walk this morning if you'll allow."

Reign smiled across the table, laying down the paper. "Of course, we shall see you at luncheon."

"Thank you." Arabella left Lord and Lady Lupton-Gage to finish their breakfast alone and went and collected her spencer, bonnet, and gloves before leaving the town house on Brook Street.

The day was sunny, yet there was a crispness to the air that hinted the Season was passing by, and it would soon be over, and the cooler seasons would arrive.

Significantly fewer people were about. She supposed most were recovering from the previous evening's balls and parties. She crossed through Grosvenor Square, down Carlos Street, then Mount Street before making Berkeley Square. Nerves fluttered in her stomach at the thought of seeing Leo again, and so soon after their interlude in the carriage.

She should not be here, of course. Visiting a gentleman without a maid was highly scandalous, but she had to see and check to ensure he was as best as he could be, considering the circumstances.

She kicked her heels across the street from his grand town house only minutes later. A highly polished carriage was parked before the home, and dallying as she was, she stayed by the park gates until an elderly, heavy-built man exited the house and climbed inside, soon rumbling his way through Mayfair.

Did that mean Leo was now alone?

Rallying every ounce of gumption, she crossed the street and banged the lion's head on the wooden door. An elderly butler dressed in black opened the door. His taut mouth and glare that seemed to run the length of his beak nose told her she was not welcome and should not be there.

"Come in, Arabella," she heard Leo call from the library.

She threw the butler a small smile, not wishing to have any bad feelings toward Leo's staff, and made her way toward the library. The room was much the same as she remembered it the last time she was here, rummaging through his desk drawers before he caught her.

Thank heavens Frederick was now settled at Lord Lupton-Gage's country estate, and he seemed to be changing his life, and for the better.

The moment she spied Leo, her footsteps faltered, and she paused halfway across the room. "I heard the news and wanted to see how you were. I'm so very sorry for your loss, Leo."

"There is no loss when it comes to my father. Do not distress yourself."

His words went against his disheveled state. Dark shadows sat beneath his eyes. His hair looked unkempt and unwashed.

Had he slept at all?

She went to him, standing before him, and without thought, sat on his lap and pulled him into her arms. "A loss or not, as your friend, I feel it is my duty to hug you right now."

Surprisingly, his arms went about her, and he held her tight, his face pooling into her shoulder. "You smell so much better than I." His words were self-deprecating, and Arabella chuckled.

"Have you slept? Had anything to eat?" She went to stand to ring the bellpull, and he drew her back onto his lap.

"My father's lawyer was here upon arriving back home last evening. I have not slept at all. He's only now just left."

"Yes, I saw him."

Leo met her eye, a small smile playing on his lips. "Yes, I saw you loitering across the road. You should not have come. If you were seen, you'd be ruined."

"I had to check on you to ensure you were well."

"I am well enough." He stood, lifting her as he went and set her on the desk. He leaned down, brushing his lips against hers so softly that she could not hold back the little mewling sigh that escaped.

"You must return home, Arabella. My home is no place for a lady."

She nodded, disappointed to leave him so soon. "I

suppose this is goodbye then. Will you return to your county estate or remain in town during your mourning?"

"I shall return to Kent. Father will be buried there in the family crypt, and then I shall return for the next Season."

Arabella supposed this was the end of their agreement. She would have to find a husband, or at least pretend to be looking for one for the remainder of the Season without his help. The idea was almost enough to make her scream with boredom.

She reached up and clasped his face in her hands. No matter how nonchalant he tried to appear at the death of his father, something was lurking deep and dark within him that left her uneasy, as if he was truly rattled, and yet refused to admit it.

"Were you close to your father? Will you miss him?"

"No, not as much as I shall miss our escapades." He reached for her, pulling her to the edge of the desk, and heat spiked through her. Warmth settled between her legs, and that delicious ache was back, begging to be sated.

Without thought, she shuffled up her gown and wrapped her legs around his waist. "We should have a goodbye, Your Grace," she teased, pulling him close. She gasped in shock when his cock, hard and ready, pressed against her mons, taunting her.

"Arabella, we can't," he groaned, his words opposite to what his hands were doing. He ripped at his falls, his cock springing against her cunny, before he edged closer, pressing into her and filling her to the hilt.

"God damn it, Arabella. You make me want things I should not."

"Yes, it is the same for me too." She lay on the desk, spread her legs wider, and watched as he thrust a second time within her aching flesh. He was so large, so thick and commanding, that she gasped aloud, reaching back to hold the edges of the desk to stop her from moving backward.

He pumped into her with such a frantic need that she could not keep pace. Her body thrummed with urgency, longing for another tremendous release, yet it did not come. Not quick enough in any case.

Leo groaned her name, pumping his seed into her, her name a plea on his lips.

She bit her lip, her body wanting more, to feel as he did, and then he pulled out, dipped to his knees, and his mouth was on her, laving her engorged, wanting flesh. Flicking the sweet, needy nubbin until she could not hold back her pleasure a moment more.

She clasped his hair, held him against her, and rolled her hips as wave after wave of incandescent pleasure spiraled, twisted, and convulsed through her.

"Leo," she gasped, moaning when he did not relent until she was fully sated.

He stood and pulled her to sit on his desk, clasping her face in his hands. "You did not think I would let you go without one last hurrah. I always satisfy, Miss Hall."

She nodded, unable to form words.

He certainly did.

TWENTY-FOUR

J ust as he said he would, Lord Wyndham left for his estate in Kent, and the next three weeks were less than pleasing and not at all as exciting as they had been when Leo had been in town.

Knowing that she could not flirt with Lord Russell to try to spark Leo's enviousness, if he indeed held when it came to her, made the Season lose its grandeur, and she could not wait for it to end.

At least at the end of the Season, Evie had asked her to visit her in Scotland, which would replace a little of the ennui until she saw Leo again.

If you see him again.

The thought was not worth thinking about, and she clutched her stomach, trying to stem the sickly nervous feeling she had whenever she thought about marrying someone else because Leo never offered.

Indeed, they could not have had so many intimate interludes, and he feel nothing. It was impossible to comprehend.

"Miss Hall, a missive has arrived for you."

Arabella set down the cup of tea she enjoyed on the back terrace of the London home and reached for the letter. "Thank you, Anne." Arabella broke the seal, recognizing the writing as that of her brother.

She pushed down the thought of him being in more trouble, of having gotten himself into strife in Derbyshire, but the further she read, the more pleased she was by his outcome.

Dearest Arabella,

I am well, and I hope this letter finds you well also. I'm writing to you first to announce that I'm to be married to the widow Noelle Fletcher, a neighbor to Lord and Lady Lupton-Gage. You will no longer need to worry about your brother, Bells, as Noelle is well situated, and I'm to come up in the world, equal to you now. I hope you travel to Derbyshire in late September to celebrate our happy day.

Frederick

Arabella laid the missive down, optimistic for her sibling that he had found a match. Her attention moved to the biscuits the cook had prepared, and her stomach seized. She ran to the terrace's side, casting her accounts onto Reign's pretty daffodils.

She fetched a handkerchief out of her pocket and dabbed at her mouth, unable to fathom what had happened, why she had been poorly.

"Arabella, are you well, my dear?"

She turned to find Reign staring at her, a deep frown

between her brows. "Come and sit with me and have some water."

Arabella sat across from Reign and fought to stop the dizziness that accompanied her episode.

"Did you eat something disagreeable? Has something upset you? Who was the letter from Anne just brought to you?"

Arabella sipped the chilled water and already felt a little better. "The missive was from Frederick. He's marrying the widow Fletcher. You know of her, do you not?"

"Oh, of course, she lives not far from our country estate. How wonderful for your brother."

"Yes, he sounds most happy, and I hope marriage will halt any of the vices he seemed to harbor here in town."

"Well, we can only hope." Reign leaned back in her chair, her interest in Arabella never waning.

"Have you been feeling ill of late? I know you have cried off attending some events."

Arabella nibbled on the ginger biscuit and considered the question. "I do not believe so. I have only been sick once, which was just now and most sporadic. I hope I'm not coming down with the ague."

"I do also." Reign pursed her lips before standing. "I shall have the cook make up a tisane for you, and perhaps a lie down upstairs is best for the remainder of the day."

Locking herself in her room to wallow over Leo seemed like a beautiful idea. She nodded. "I think I shall take up your advice and do that. Thank you, Reign."

"Do let me know if you're ill again." Reign threw her a reassuring smile, yet there was concern, a shadow in her gaze that left Arabella curious.

Did she think something much more troubling was

befalling her? She hoped her pining for Lord Wyndham had not caused her to become ill.

She sighed and put down the biscuit, no longer feeling up to eating it. She would return upstairs now and lie back down. The Maddigon's Rout was this evening and a must-attend due to Lord and Lady Maddigon being good friends with Lord and Lady Lupton-Gage.

If only Leo were present, that would make attending worthwhile for her.

L eo watched as his father's coffin was interred in the family mausoleum. No family or friends attended. No one but himself and the local vicar. His father did not like many people, including his son, so Leo doubted he would be displeased by the turnout. He'd never held any enjoyment in life; his funeral may as well be as miserable as he had been.

The vicar again gave his condolences before leaving him alone with his father. He narrowed his eyes on the casket that would soon be interred, glad it was over. Not that he'd always held his father in such little regard. Early in his life, he'd once looked up to the powerful duke, but when he had changed, morphed into a monster that he, along with his mother, feared, he lost all respect and could not wait to be free of him.

And now he was truly free, yet fear lurked at the back of his mind of how people change. How they can appear calm, eloquent, and pleasing and change into someone that had they looked into a mirror Leo doubted would have recognized themselves.

He turned on his heel and left the mausoleum at the top of a hill overlooking the estate. A place that he supposed he, too, would end up one day, but no wife or child would stand before his grave, mourning him.

No, that was not a future he cared to achieve.

Not even with Arabella?

The thought floated through his mind, and as usual, disconcerting, chaotic thoughts and feelings followed it. He cared for her. He liked her very much and wanted her with a longing that often took his breath away, but he would not make her endure his life.

What if he turned into a man similar to what his father had become? What if he turned on a dime and thought it suitable to strike her when they argued or belt his child for speaking out of turn?

He grabbed his horse's reins and mounted, kicking his horse into a canter to escape the mausoleum as fast as possible. He rarely visited there other than to lay flowers on his mother's final resting place.

He could almost feel sorry for her having to be so close to his father once again. Thank heavens she could not know of it.

No matter how disappointing the *ton* would be, he would not mourn him for long. A week or two at most, but he deserved little else. He would return to London, take up his reins as one of the most scandalous men in town, and enjoy his life.

Just as he had been doing up until meeting Arabella.

But what to do about their agreement?

Surely, Lord Russell would offer marriage soon, and he would be able to stop thinking of Arabella as his. Stop craving her as much as he did.

She did not deserve to live under a cloud of the unknown. To be his wife, marry him, love him as he imagined she would, only to be as disappointed and heartbroken when at five and thirty, only seven years from now, the same madness descended on him as it had his father, leaving her beaten and battered.

No, he could not do that to her. Not to any woman.

He would return to London, notify Miss Hall that their agreement was at an end, and look to seeking his pleasures elsewhere, just as he had before.

She would marry and fall in love, and all would be well. She was certainly more popular in the *ton* now that she had his help, which was what they had set out to do in the first place.

Guilt prickled low in his belly, and he shook the emotion aside. He should not feel shame. He had done right by her when he could have ignored the insult from Lord Spencer in the park that day and allowed her to continue paying for her brother's misguided life.

But he had not. He had been a gentleman for the first time and had helped an unfortunate debutante become a fortunate one.

Miss Hall would understand, and they would part as friends as they had started.

No harm nor foul.

CHAPTER

TWENTY-FIVE

Two weeks later, Arabella had the awful sinking feeling that something was amiss. She refused to put a name on the fear that harbored in her mind, but it was there, forever lurking, taunting her until she thought she would go mad.

She was late for her courses, and if they continued not to arrive, she would have to tell Reign and face disappointing her guardian.

Arabella smiled as Lord Russell, whom she now called her friend, had finally asked for Lady Southwell's hand in the last week, and she had agreed. Thanks to Arabella, with Lord Russell's help, she made the widow outlandishly covetous, so much so that she believed herself in love with Lord Russell and wanted him.

But now, there was no one she could use to make Lord Wyndham envious, not that he attended any balls or dinners. She had not heard a word from him since he left for his country estate.

Although she had heard whispers, and he had arrived in London three days before. Yet he had not called on her.

Not that she expected him to attend society events, but she had thought he would call at Lord and Lady Lupton-Gage's town house. They were friends before anything else happened between them, and she needed to speak to him to see if he believed her fears were founded.

She bit her lip, the nausea ever churning in her stomach a reminder of what that conversation would be about. Perhaps she was making herself sick over it, and nothing else was going on with her.

Perhaps it was all in her mind...

Do not be a fool, Arabella. You know what is wrong with you, and you can do nothing about it. You're in trouble, ruined...

A footman passed with a tray of champagne, and she reached for a glass, sipping it to calm her fraught mind.

She could leave, buy a small cottage far away from London, and live off the money she inherited. She did not need a husband. She may be ruined and shunned by people who knew her, but surely she could make up some anecdote about who she was to the village she would live in. It could not be so hard to disappear and start a new life.

Her stomach chose that moment to twist and churn, and she excused herself, moving toward the ballroom door. Thankfully, Reign crossed her path before she left.

"Lady Lupton-Gage, I'm so glad to find you. I think I ought to return home. A sudden headache, unfortunately."

Reign frowned and linked her arm with her. "I shall come with you. In any case, his lordship has headed off to his club, and there is nothing to keep me here. We shall have a little chat in the carriage, as there's something I've been meaning to discuss with you in any case."

Arabella nodded, pleased for the company, but the moment she sat across the carriage from her ladyship, the concern etched on Reign's face told her this conversation was not one she wanted to partake in.

"You've often been ill, and your courses are late, my dear. Is there something you wish to tell me? I will not judge you, I promise. I only mean to help."

Arabella sighed and slumped into the squabs like a weight lifted from her. "I'm so ashamed of myself. I thought a future was possible for me, but it was not. I was wrong about so many things, and now I think I'm ruined."

"Who is the father, Arabella? I know it must be one of two men courting with you, but your lack of upset over Lord Russell's recent betrothal tells me it is Lord Wyndham's child you carry."

Arabella swiped at the tears flowing and cursed herself a silly, naive fool. "He will not marry me. He's told me he does not want a wife, now or ever, including children. I think it would be best to leave, move to a rural cottage, and raise this child alone. London can forget that I was ever here."

"No, Lord Wyndham is a grown man and more than capable, just as you are, to know the risks you both took being intimate. Lord Lupton-Gage will request his attendance as soon as possible, and you shall talk to him about what is afoot. But know this, Arabella, you will not be ruined. His lordship and I will not allow it."

Arabella wished she could believe Reign, but she could not. The thought of telling Leo of her pregnancy was not a truth she wanted to disclose. He would despise her if she forced marriage onto him, not of his choosing. The marriage would be worse than had she disappeared into the country, never to be seen again.

"I shall speak to him, but I do not hold out much hope, my lady. He's a duke now, and I'm a woman from servitude.

When it comes to making anyone do what may be right, when one is high enough in society to choose if that is what they wish or not, it is another matter entirely."

"Lord Wyndham will do the right thing. He's a gentleman, after all. We must trust in that," Reign said, seemingly ending their conversation.

And yet Arabella heard the tremble of unease in her voice that only doubled her fear that deep down, Lady Lupton-Gage knew too that her days in society were finite.

T he following afternoon, Leo tapped his fingers against his leg while waiting for Miss Hall to attend him in Lady Lupton-Gage's private parlor. Nerves twisted his stomach into knots, and he fought down the trepidation, the expectation of seeing Arabella again.

It had been almost a month since he parted London, and had glimpsed her pretty face.

That was the only reason he had missed her. That and the desire that bubbled up within him was the only reason he wished to see her again. It was not because he liked her far more than he ought.

He was not the type of gentleman who fell for women.

The door opened, and he stood, forcing himself to breathe when he realized he was holding his breath. Arabella entered the room and closed the door, her attention not once diverting to him.

Look at me, damn it, he wanted to demand across the room, and then at length she did, she glanced up, and their eyes met.

A bolt of desire, longing, and wanting to hear her voice assailed him, and he cursed himself a fool.

You will only make her life miserable...

"Miss Hall," he said, throwing her a small smile that he hoped put any of her nerves at seeing him again at ease.

"Your Grace." Her words caught him off guard, and she dipped into a curtsy before joining him on the settee.

They sat and did not say a word for what felt like an eternity. "I hope I find you well. I have meant to call to discuss our association, which I'm sorry about, but I think it must end."

Her wide gaze stared at him, and he wondered if she would blink anytime soon.

"Even though I've heard Lord Russell has asked Lady Southwell to marry him, I'm certain others will now step forward and show interest. You no longer require my help. I'm certain of it." Leo watched for Arabella to move, to say anything, but she paled to the point that he thought she might cast up her accounts.

She reached for a glass of water a footman had left for him upon arrival and took several sips. "There is something I must tell you, Your Grace."

He nodded and waited as patiently as he could before her continued silence almost drove him to insanity.

Not to mention, having her so close again, the sweet scent of vanilla teasing his senses, reminding him of how she felt and tasted when he kissed her, was almost too much to deny.

"Arabella, are you going to tell me what you want, or am I going to sit and guess what you wish to say?" he teased, trying to make light of this very odd conversation.

"I do not think you'll be pleased, and I must admit I'm a little apprehensive about telling you."

Her pallor worsened, and a repulsive thought flittered through his mind that he lurched back from her on the chair. "Do not say it," he warned, unprepared, not ready, not for anything if she said what he feared she would.

Tears welled in her eyes, and he knew. Deep in his innards, the dread churned, taunted, and mocked him for a fool, a rogue who had ruined all his plans, his promises to himself.

"Leo, I'm sorry, but I believe I'm expecting."

TWENTY-SIX

"And now you wish to marry?"

Arabella flinched at the cold, cutting tone in which Leo delivered that question. Considering the circumstances, she nodded, not knowing what else she could want. "I know it is not what you wished, and I did not want to entangle you like this. I do not know what I was thinking, but I did not plan for this to happen any more than you would have."

Leo stood and paced back and forth toward the settee and unlit fire. He ran a hand through his hair, mumbling responses she could not make out. Was it so very terrible that she was having his child? She supposed it was, if he did not care for her at all, and what they had shared the past weeks was her fanciful dreams that only she reciprocated. Was not what he wanted and he'd meant every word when he'd disclosed his wishes.

"I cannot be a father. There must be other choices."

Arabella gasped, unable to hide her stupefaction at his words. What was he thinking? He could not mean what he was saying. It was the shock he was experiencing and nothing else. He could not be so heartless.

"I understand that this is a lot to take in, to think about, but I'm already some weeks along, and if you are not going to marry me, then I shall have to make alternate arrangements." Like leaving London, fleeing the city, and all the heartbreak it would remind her of should he not do the right thing.

Which right at this moment, she did not think he would.

"You should make alternate arrangements. That's exactly what you should do," he said, his words laced with distaste.

"Any suggestions, Your Grace?" she replied with more venom than she thought she ever would. "We made the mistake, and you can be part of this child's life, or you will not be. The choice is yours. But right at this moment I think it is best that you leave."

He stopped pacing and stared at her like she had grown two heads. Leo looked downright wretched. The fear lurking in his eyes made little sense, not really. Yes, having a child was scary, but she was early enough in the pregnancy that should they marry, no one ever need to know they had been intimate before their vows.

"You will have to leave London this week." His demanding words spiked her ire more.

"I shall leave when I'm ready," Arabella returned, defiant. "For a man who ruts his way around London quite often, your fear of children, which I should remind you, is a possibility when you keep putting your manhood into women, is quite alarming. Or do you not know what happens when men and women make love? Are you so wicked that perhaps you do not care?"

He scoffed. "We are not in love." Leo walked over to where a whisky decanter sat and poured himself a glass, downing it in one swallow. "It has never happened before, and I merely hoped that I was infertile." He poured another glass and downed it a second time. "Are you certain the child is mine?"

Arabella stood and walked to the door. "Get out. I think our association, friendship, whatever this was between us," she gestured, "is now at an end. How dare you even ask me that question? I'm not the one who is the whore here, Your Grace. Perhaps you should look in the mirror above that decanter from which you're drinking like water and take a long, hard look at who is staring back."

"You cannot speak to me like that. I'm the Duke Carnavon. No one insults me, especially a woman like you."

"Like me?" His words hit her like he had physically dealt the blow himself. "Leave," she managed, unable to form another word due to the lump in her throat.

"Arabella, I'm sorry. I did not mean..."

"Out. Now. Leave this very moment. I never wish to lay eyes on you ever again."

He placed his crystal tumbler down and strode from the room, not saying a word as he passed her at the threshold.

Arabella slammed the door in his wake and, like in a trance, walked to the settee and slumped upon it.

The conversation had gone differently than she had hoped. She had prayed he would understand. He was partly to blame for their predicament, after all. But to accuse her of trying to trap him, that had not been a fear until now.

Of course, she wanted to marry him, but not in that way. She had hoped he would fall in love with her, want her as his duchess because he could not live without her.

What a fool she had been, thinking there was more to

their friendship than there was. She had been a pretty piece of meat and nothing else. She would never forgive him for his cruelty.

Not for as long as she lived.

Leo heard the front door to his town house slam against the foyer wall, rattling the chandelier before the quick, determined footsteps followed across the tiled floor.

Lord Lupton-Gage burst into his office, and Leo leaned back in his chair, a glass of whisky in his hand, one of many he'd partaken in since leaving Arabella several hours ago.

Broken, ashamed, scared, furiously angry. With himself.

And who could blame her for how she was likely feeling? He'd acted an ass, and he knew she would never forgive him for his cutting remarks.

"You will marry her, or we'll meet at dawn."

Leo waved Lupton-Gage's words aside and smirked instead, more than willing to have another argument, if only to further his misery.

A child?

The thought made him want to vomit. Of all the horrible, unfortunate outcomes of their union, this was it.

"I will not be, and nothing you say will change the fact. I will not meet you at dawn. There is no proof the child is mine. I shall not lower myself to dignify your absurd request."

"You know Miss Hall's character. What is wrong with you, man?"

"I will not be saddled with a wife or child," he declared yet again, wondering how many times he would have to say it before the knot in his stomach stopped churning, telling him he was immoral, that he was doing wrong by Arabella. "I helped Miss Hall become favored in society, any more than that I shall deny." He was a bastard. Where were these words coming from? He sounded awfully like his father—cold, calculated, and dismissive.

When had he become like his sire? He'd always strived to be the opposite of him, yet now, he was the same.

Damn himself to hell.

"That choice was removed the moment you were intimate with Miss Hall. You must marry her, do the right thing, Carnavon. For all your rakish tendencies, I have never known you to be as cruel as you are now."

He shrugged, wanting Lupton-Gage out of his house. To stop saying words that prickled the guilt that ate him alive. "Well then, you do not know me very well." He gestured toward the door and leaned back in his chair. "This conversation is over. You may leave."

"I will ruin you should you destroy Miss Hall. A duke or not, I shall ensure everyone knows of your misdeed, even if Miss Hall and her truth becomes known. Do not make this mistake, Carnavon. You will regret it."

Leo scoffed, picked up his whisky, and finished it. "I doubt that very much. I was honest and disclosed my stance on such a future with Miss Hall. She was interested in Lord Russell, if you must know, never me."

"And you slept with her," Lupton-Gage spat back.

"We may have enjoyed an intimate moment or two, but it was not me she wanted, that you must know. She will be happier married to another or to leave London as she suggested. I will not stand in her way."

"You're a fool," Lupton-Gage stated, turning on his heel to leave. "She never wanted Russell. She's in love with you, has been from the first moment you helped her in the park, and you're a bastard to think she would be intimate with anyone but the man she loved. I suggest you consider this conversation and what you've learned before making a mistake that could haunt you with regret for the rest of your life."

Leo doubted any of that and stared at Lupton-Gage until he left. He ran a hand over his face, attempting to clear his mind, but it was of no use. All his thoughts were on Arabella, the child she carried, and that he would never see her again.

Fear curdled in his mind, and he shuddered, unable to comprehend, to imagine being a father. How does one become a good parent when one suffered such a horrendous upbringing on their own?

He could not. She would be better away from him for her own sake and sanity.

Forever.

CHAPTER
TWENTY-SEVEN

Several days later, Leo was walking through his town house on Berkeley Square, drinking a fine aged Scotch, talking to the many guests who were enjoying his night of revelry, and yet, something was amiss.

He was amiss.

This life was amiss.

Nothing was as it was supposed to be. The entertainments that once gave him so much enjoyment now seemed less polished and amusing, less erotic. In fact, they downright felt monotonous.

Although he smiled and laughed at the remarks of his guests and the innuendo they voiced, none of it was entertaining.

He was in grave peril.

All he could think about was Arabella—their last conversation and how he had been an utter, mitigating bastard to her.

How could he have dared ask her if he was the father of their child? Of course, he was. With every kiss, touch, and look she bestowed upon him, he knew she had been falling in love with him.

That she adored him above all others.

That he had ignored her feelings and pretended they were not there was not her fault. They were there, and not just for her, and he knew the entire time, and now he had lost her.

She would never forgive him, as he could not forgive himself.

Tell her why you were scared of the commitment, Leo. Do not lose her now.

He should listen to the warning voice in his head or Lord Lupton-Gage. Go directly to Brook Street and demand to speak to her, even at this late hour of the night.

He had not heard from Lord Lupton-Gage again, but he knew he was at work. For surprisingly, as threatened, he had not received any invitations to society balls or dinners.

Perhaps the marquess had more clout in society than he had given him credit, even with Leo being a duke.

Not that he cared for the invitations, but he had found himself more than once wondering what Arabella was doing. Was she still attending balls and parties? Was she trying to find a husband who would marry her, even if she now carried his child?

The thought made his blood run cold, and he knew he had to go to her. To make amends and seek forgiveness.

Tomorrow, first thing, he would call on her and try to make her see why he said the things he had, dismissing her like she was a nobody.

He started toward his rooms, inwardly cringing at their interaction. So cold and final.

How she must loathe him.

His eye caught the clock on the ballroom mantel, and he

noted the time—nine o'clock, still early by society's standards. Most of the *ton* would be just heading out to their gatherings.

Instead of heading to his room to hide from his guests, he headed for the door, ordering his carriage posthaste.

It did not take long to arrive, and he was soon ensconced inside, heading toward Brook Street only to arrive and see Lord and Lady Lupton-Gage, accompanied by Arabella, drive off.

"Follow that carriage," he ordered his driver, who hastily flicked the horse's reins, and the carriage lurched forward, following the marquess's vehicle.

The carriage rolled to a halt before Viscount Billington's town house. From afar he watched Arabella alight and make her way indoors, along with the many other guests attending the ball.

He greeted Lord and Lady Billington, relieved not to be sent on his way. Once inside, it did not take him long to see where Arabella went. She followed meekly behind her guardians as they made their way through the throng of guests in the ballroom.

He stood at the side of the room for several minutes, watching Arabella, hating himself a little more each time he noted the sadness and disappointment on her features.

He had done that to her. He had made her feel wretched.

If it were his life mission, he would ensure he never saw that wretchedness on her features again.

You love her, admit it...

The thought halted his steps, and he paused, startled by his mind's admission.

Did he love her? Was that the emotion, the guilt, the fear, the shame that had plagued him these past days?

154

Was it because he loved her, too? More than the fear of the unknown, his fear of being as bad a father as his had been?

He stepped toward her, determined to right the wrong he had caused, and he would not return home until he had repaired his mistake.

Arabella sipped a glass of Ratafia. Thankful the past two days she had not bled anymore, and the doctor had assured her all was well and there was nothing wrong.

Not that they had told the doctor of their fears she had been pregnant, which in the end did not seem to be the case.

Although she could not understand the nausea that had persisted these past weeks. Mayhap, she had worried herself sick over Leo and had brought it on herself.

Had her worries caused her not to bleed at her usual time of the month? Or had she been pregnant and merely lost the baby? Either way, she was sorry if the latter had been the case. No matter what Leo wanted or did not want, she had wished for the child.

She sipped her drink and almost choked as Leo appeared before her, his hair askew and a shadow of a beard on his face, and yet, as usual, his clothing was as immaculate as his breeding.

A pang of regret tore through her. How she longed for him still. They had been friends before anything else, but now she did not know what or how she felt about him.

Their last conversation had been telling, and she was still reeling from what he had said.

"Lord and Lady Lupton-Gage, Miss Hall, a pleasure as always." The duke kept his attention on her, and nerves settled in her stomach at the determination she read in his eyes.

"Miss Hall, would you take a turn around the room with me? There are some things we need to discuss."

"A little late for that, is it not?" Lord Lupton-Gage said, his tone one of disapproval.

"Just a quick turn will be acceptable," Lady Lupton-Gage interjected, linking her arm with her husband's.

Arabella, not wanting to cause a scene, nodded. Leo clasped her hand and placed it on his arm before escorting her on their turn.

"I owe you an apology, Arabella. I'm sorry for how I spoke to you the last time we met. I've acted atrociously, but I would like a chance to explain."

"Explain," Arabella scoffed, her pride still stinging after he accused her of being a lightskirt who gave her body away to anyone who was a male and titled in London. "I look forward to hearing how you're going to explain away everything you said."

He looked at her, and she stared back, wishing she could reach out, touch him, kiss him, and make all that had passed between them better, but she could not.

He had hurt her more than he could ever understand, and she wasn't confident she could forgive him for it.

"I did not mean anything that I said. Your news last week pitched me through a loop of fear, and I acted out. I hit out and hurt you, and I'm sorry. I have never had to face such a possibility, so I did not know what to do."

"Well, you could have acted like a gentleman and offered for my hand since I was carrying your child," she said, ignoring the fact that she had no proof if that was true or not anymore, but still, she could not think of any other reason why her courses would have been so out of sync.

"I'm asking now, here at this ball, for you to be my wife. I'm sorry, truly, but I did not have a good upbringing. I never had a father to show me what it was like to love and care. I panicked." He paused, stopping her near several pedestals of roses and climbing ivy used for decoration. "What do you mean since I was carrying your child? Why past tense?" he asked.

Arabella swallowed the lump in her throat and raised her chin. "My courses came the day after you called, and the doctor has inspected me and says everything is as it should be, but there is no baby. So you are quite free to do as you please, Your Grace. In fact, do you not have a party of your own this evening you should be attending? Perhaps you ought to run back to your amusing friends and leave me alone."

She went to walk away, but he grabbed her arm, pulling her to a stop. "You're not expecting?" he whispered, the concern on his features almost believable if she had not heard his horrible, caustic words a week before.

"No, I am not. So I shall find a husband as I should have many weeks ago instead of risking everything to try to make you fall in love with me." Arabella wrenched her arm free, shaking her head, hating herself even now for wanting what she could not have. Should not want. "What a waste of time you have been. A rake makes the best husband, they say. I think in your case, Your Grace, the opposite would be true."

TWENTY-EIGHT

"Miss Arabella Hall, I love you."

The words echoed through the room and herself, halting her steps. The music lulled, and the many conversations in the ballroom ceased. The shock and interest on everyone's faces, as they turned to see who had made such an outrageous, personal state-ment, increased further when they realized it was the Duke of Carnavon, declaring himself in the most public of ways.

Arabella turned and faced Leo, unable to believe he would shout such words across the room so forcefully, so proudly.

He loved her?

"I'm sorry, Arabella. I'm so sorry. Please say you'll forgive me." He did not move, content it would seem, to carry the conversation on as publicly as he'd started it.

Arabella glanced about and noted the many interested eyes. She did not want them to know what they had done. The risks they had taken that had left her on the brink of ruin. And yet, she also wanted to hear him say more, possibly grovel at her feet. She certainly deserved a little begging after what he had put her through.

"Sorry for what, Your Grace?" she asked, crossing her arms and waiting for him to reply. If he desperately wanted to disclose his failings, he could do so before the *ton*.

"For failing you. When you truly needed a friend, I let you down at the very first moment. I've always been selfish," he said, coming to stand before her. "If you would allow me to explain my actions and why I acted the way I did, I hope you'll find it in your heart to forgive me."

Several ladies nearby sighed at his words, and as much as Arabella tried to hold on to her hurt, annoyance, and anger, she also supposed he deserved to explain why he had acted the way he had.

She did not have to believe or forgive his sins, but would hear him out.

"Very well, I shall hear what you have to say."

Without a word, he clasped her hand and walked them both from the ballroom before the startled eyes of everyone. But she was wrong if Arabella thought he would find a quiet place within Lord and Lady Billington's home to discuss what had transpired between them a week before.

He escorted her to the town house's front door and ordered his carriage. "I cannot leave here with you. Everyone knows we walked out of the ball together, and if I were not ruined before, I most certainly will be after this."

"I'm hoping that after we speak, you'll be the next Duchess of Carnavon, so it will not matter."

Arabella rolled her eyes at his highhandedness, yet a part of her thrilled at the prospect of being married to him, to be the only woman ever to warm his bed again.

And she would be. She would not settle for anything less.

"You are very sure of yourself." Arabella thanked a footman who handed her shawl to her before she followed Leo out of the town house to climb into the carriage.

"Drive around until I say otherwise," Leo called to the driver prior to following her inside and enclosing them in the abundant space of the ducal carriage.

They sat in silence for several turns of the wheel on the cobbled street, and damn her sinful soul, the memory of what they had done in the ducal carriage taunted her mind. The feel of his desire, his need for her, the delicious slide of his manhood as he took her forcefully made her ache between the legs.

How could she want him so when she was still so very angry with him?

"Well, you have me here now. I suggest you explain why you were being such a word grubber." Arabella ignored his flinch at her scathing words, but she needed him to understand not all was forgiven, even if he did declare his love so publicly.

He took a deep breath and stared out the window, and she could see he was gathering his thoughts. "I left home as soon as I was old enough. I came to London and promised myself that I would never live a day that was not full of laughter, pleasure, joy, everything that my childhood was not."

"Well, you certainly have become very successful at that way of living." She watched him, noted sadness flittered through his moss-colored eyes, and decided to mind her manners just a little.

"You had a difficult childhood," she stated, not a question.

He nodded, continuing to stare out the window. "My

mother was a sweetheart, too good for my cold, toxic father, but she died when I was young, and so I was left to his devices—those being to be cruel, hard, temperamental, and violent as often and as much as he liked. I do not think there was a day from the age of over five that I did not get spanked. Those spankings turned to floggings when I hit the age of ten, and by the time I was eighteen, I could not stand it anymore. I knew I had to leave, or one of us would end up dead. I fled to London, and I lived as I saw fit. I would not allow pain in any form to touch me, and I fell into a dissolute life, of balls and parties, of nights of endless pleasure. Still, the moment I saw you steal into my library, I was aware my life as I knew it was about to change."

Arabella fought to understand, to not go to him after hearing how his father had been. Even as a servant, she had never been mistreated. To be unloved by one's parent and assaulted verbally and physically was a horror she could not imagine.

How awful his life must have been, even if he were also so very fortunate in other ways.

"I've been selfish. I can see that now. I pretended to help you in society, but the moment I had you, the first time we kissed, I knew I would use you up as much as I could before you were no longer mine. I was wrong. I put you at risk and then blamed you for all the troubles our actions brought upon ourselves. I'm so sorry, Arabella. I did not mean anything I said to you at Lord and Lady Lupton-Gage's home last week. I panicked, felt trapped, and hit out, and I should not have."

"No, you should not have. I never intended to trap you. I would have been happy to disappear and never see you again, but Reign talked me into being honest with you to give you the choice. She thought you would do the right thing..."

"And I let you all down by doing the worst imaginable." He came and sat beside her, reaching for her hands. "I never knew kindness or love, not after my mother passed. Instead, I learned to defend, protect myself, and surround myself with a carefree life without responsibilities or fear. When you told me what you believed, that you were carrying my child, I panicked. I do not wish to be a bad father or husband. Therefore, I never intended to become one because I was scared I would fail. I did not want my child to have an upbringing like mine. Or my wife to flinch whenever I raised my hand."

"You thought just because of how your father was, that you would follow in his footsteps?" Arabella shook her head, hating that Leo believed such a heinous thing. "I do not think you would have been like him at all. I think you may have surprised yourself with how exemplary you were."

"Arabella," he whispered. "I hope what I said, my treatment, did not cause you to lose our child. I could never forgive myself if I had done this to you."

"You have been honest with me, and now I shall be honest with you and say there is no way to know. I do not even know if I was pregnant, just that some of the signs I was portraying hinted it to be so. But we will never know for sure." She paused, wishing she could tell him he had not, but she did not know. "I was distraught. Your words hurt me, but there is no way to know, and I cannot live with the anger and hatred I felt for you for the last few days. I decided to find a husband, stop the games we have been playing, and leave you in the past. I will not make you do what you do not want. That would be unfair of me."

"I do not want you to leave me in the past. I want you to be my future. I want us to be each other's tomorrow and all the days after. Please tell me I have not lost you through my foolish, selfish actions. Tell me that I'm not too late."

"I do not know if I can," she said.

CHAPTER
TWENTY-NINE

Panic seized Leo, and for several moments, he could not think of what to do or say to make Arabella understand. But then, what could he say for her to understand his misbegotten behavior? There was no excuse. Not even his woeful childhood gave him reason to speak to her as he had. He deserved everything and anything that Arabella wished to mete out to him.

"I know my past is no excuse, but it is all I have, my only explanation. I panicked."

Arabella considered his words. He held her hand, stroking the soft flesh of her palm, hoping, praying that she would forgive him. "Please give me a chance to make it up to you. I want you to be my wife. My duchess. Tell me that I've not put everything into disarray between us and you will not have me now."

She sighed, her lips thinning into a displeased line. "I do not want you to marry me out of pity, Leo. I think that would be far worse than any other type of union. If you have never wanted a wife or children, I do not want to force you into a situation that you may regret and resent me for years to come. I would prefer someone else if that were to be my fate."

"No, Arabella, no. I do not want you to have that kind of marriage. I want you to marry me. I love you. These past days have been hell, and now, to learn what you have been going through and what we could have possibly lost, I'm beyond ashamed of how I reacted and spoke. I ought to be horsewhipped."

A scolding his father had enjoyed dishing out, and one he would prefer not to endure again, but if it were to make Arabella look at him as she once had, love him as he hoped she once did, he would suffer such a fate.

"You hurt me by what you said, terribly so. I've never felt so ashamed and small and unworthy in my life. How could you be so cold to me?"

He wrenched her into his arms, holding her close, trying to force the sadness out of her soul by holding her tight. "I'm a bastard, that is why. I have no excuse. Not even my fear of being a father should have given me leave to speak to you. If you will not have me, I understand and will let you go, but know that it will only be you I want. My friend, my lover, my Arabella."

She did not hold him back for a time, and despair taunted him that he was too late. But then, slowly, her arms slipped about his waist and held him tight. He kissed her temple, holding her as if he would never let her go, and he would not, not if she allowed it.

"If I have to say it a million times a day until you believe me, I'm so sorry, Arabella. I love you. Marry me. Let me prove to you I mean every word I speak."

She looked up at him, and in the shadowed carriage, he could see her eyes glistened with tears. He dipped his head, wanting to take away her pain, to kiss her, to replace the sadness with anything but that emotion.

She did not shy away but kissed him back with a tenderness that left him reeling. She tasted like wine and smelled like vanilla.

They sank onto the squabs. Leo slipped his hand beneath her gown, tracing her long, soft legs. She squirmed beneath him, her breathy moan telling him she liked his touch.

He grazed her mons and rolled two fingers against her needy nubbin.

"Leo," she gasped, lifting her bottom to seek his touch.

"Lie back and enjoy, my darling." He teased her flesh and used the moisture pooling at her core to create a delicious friction she loved. He entered her with his finger, teasing, fucking, rolling her womanhood until she was gasping for release.

"Oh yes, do not stop."

"I did not plan on doing so," he said, unable to deny himself. He dipped his head beneath her skirts and suckled her sweet quim. Flicked her with his tongue but twice, and that was all it took.

Her fingers clasped his hair, and pain shot through his skull at the force in which she held him. She rocked against his face and enjoyed every tremor that weaved through her body as he brought her to release.

"Leo," she screamed, holding him firmly until satisfied.

Never in his life had he ever felt as used and wonderfully so as he did right at that moment. He loved bringing her to release, making her feel as wonderful as she always made him feel.

Once their hearts had calmed, he pulled her to sit before slipping off the seat to kneel before her. "Marry me, Arabella," he said, reaching into his breast pocket and pulling out the ducal diamond ring his mother once wore. "I do not lie when I say I love you. I have never said those words to another living thing in my life. I adore you, love you, and need you to be mine. As I want to be yours, please say you'll marry me."

She stared at him, her gaze dipping to the ring, her mouth agape. "I do not know what to say," she whispered.

He slipped the ring on her finger and squeezed her hands. "Say yes, Arabella."

The smile he loved and had missed blossomed on her face, and she nodded, her eyes glassy with unshed tears. "Well, since you're on your knees and begging, I suppose it would only be right if I said yes."

He chuckled, knowing that when it came to Arabella, he would always bow down to her. "So that is a yes?"

"Yes... Yes, I shall marry you because I love you too."

Leo had never heard those words from anyone other than his mama, which was too many years ago to remember. The rush of emotions that swamped him caught him off guard, and he balked as Arabella's pretty visage swam in his vision.

"Are you crying?" The shock in her voice mirrored his.

"No, of course not. I merely have dust in my eye." He came and sat beside her and blinked rapidly. He'd never cried in his life, not even when his father had belted the living life out of him, and yet here he was, emotional because Arabella had said that she loved him too.

He knew her answer meant everything, but even he did not know how much that everything was.

"It's okay to cry, Leo, just as it's okay to love and be loved."

Her words undid him, and he could not swallow the

lump in his throat. All he could do was nod and meet her gaze.

"I'm sorry for everything that you suffered to make you want to hide yourself away from ever being hurt. And I'm sorry for my part in our messy courtship, if one could call it that. But I cannot regret winning your heart and hand. I adore you, Leo. So very much, and I will endeavor to make you know that for the rest of your life."

He smiled and reached for her again, holding her close and rocking her in his arms. "I promise never to let you down, Arabella. Never again will I ever hurt you. I give you my word."

She hugged him tighter, her reply muffled against his shoulder. "And I you. Forever."

EPILOGUE

Eight years later, Kent

Arabella waddled into the drawing room, her steps halting where several settees and tables once sat before the large marble fireplace.

Instead of the fashionable, comfortable furnishings she had carefully chosen upon their marriage set out just as she planned, they sat upturned, stacked together in a hodge-podge of a layout and blankets and sheets thrown over it all.

Giggles and squeals of laughter, including that of her husband, came from the monstrosity of the fort they had built, and she went and sat on a hard wooden chair nearby, much to her very pregnant body's dismay.

"Leo, you know it would make much more sense if you built them a fort outside in the trees instead of making our delightful boys these forts in our living room daily."

"But where would the fun be in that," her husband's muffled voice said before his head poked out from between two leg chairs, the sheet covering his head like a veil. "We remain dry inside, and the room is big enough, and the Aubusson rug in which we create this fort gives a most comfortable place to lay one's head."

Arabella chuckled, stroking her stomach at her husband's many excuses. Truly, in the past years since she had given birth to their first child, she had watched with love and affection as he had rectified his childhood with his boys, enjoying playing and laughing just as a child should.

Just as he should have been given the opportunity and had not been.

"Very well," she conceded. "It does not look like I shall change your mind." Arabella went over to where she thought the entrance might be. She leaned down and lifted the blanket, and before her were her three beating hearts, her two sons and husband, who were lying on a bed of pillows from who knows which room, an array of books stacked all about them. "Is there room in there for one more?"

"Of course, Mama," her eldest son Samuel shouted, patting a space beside him for her.

She kneeled and crawled as best she could between them. "Mama, you can fit between me and Samuel," her youngest son, Harrison, said, his little voice the sweetest sound in the world.

She nestled between them and wrapped her arms around her boys, and Leo read them a nursery rhyme. The baby kicked inside as if he or she, too, wished to join in with the revelry, and soon the baby would as well.

All too soon...

How she hoped it would be a girl, a little flower to add to their bouquet.

Leo finished the story, and the boys started to explore the fort more, the many tunnels Leo had created for them. "You have outdone yourself this time. How long do you suppose the furniture will be unavailable in this room, do you think?" she asked in a teasing note.

Leo laid his head in her lap, the wicked, playful smile she adored more than life itself taunting her as usual. "A week or two at most. I have designs for the billiard room. I think the table in there is perfect to make a fort grander than any I've ever made."

"I think that would be a wonderful idea." If only to get her comfortable settees back, especially considering her condition.

"Arabella," Leo said, his tone serious.

She ran her hand through his hair and met his gaze. "Yes, Leo?" she asked him.

"Thank you for everything. I have never been so happy, and I know I have you to thank for this wonderful life."

His words sparked an emotion that she often experienced being heavily pregnant, and she swiped at her eyes, not wanting the boys to think anything was wrong, for it was not. Everything was right. So perfectly right.

"Thank you for being gallant and helping me in the park that day. All this life could be attributed to you being a wonderful man, even when you thought you were not."

"No, it was down to you. I love you so much, my darling wife."

"I love you more."

"No, I love you more," Samuel shouted from somewhere in the fort.

"No, I love Mama and Papa more. I say it more than you do," Harrison argued.

Arabella laughed, and Leo sat up, clasping her face. "No, I love you all the most," he whispered, only for her to hear.

She smiled, leaning forward to kiss him and to show him, without words, she felt the same.

Always.

DON'T MISS TAMARA'S OTHER ROMANCE SERIES

My Reckless Earl

Brazen Rogue

The Notorious Lord Sin

Wicked in My Bed

League of Unweddable Gentlemen

Tempt Me, Your Grace

Hellion at Heart

Dare to be Scandalous

To Be Wicked With You

Kiss Me, Duke

The Marquess is Mine

Kiss the Wallflower

A Midsummer Kiss

A Kiss at Mistletoe

A Kiss in Spring

To Fall For a Kiss

A Duke's Wild Kiss

To Kiss a Highland Rose

To Marry a Rogue

Only an Earl Will Do

Only a Duke Will Do

Only a Viscount Will Do

Only a Marquess Will Do

Only a Lady Will Do

Lords of London

To Bedevil a Duke

To Madden a Marquess

To Tempt an Earl

To Vex a Viscount

To Dare a Duchess

To Marry a Marchioness

Royal House of Atharia

To Dream of You

A Royal Proposition

Forever My Princess

A Time Traveler's Highland Love

To Conquer a Scot

To Save a Savage Scot

To Win a Highland Scot

A Stolen Season

A Stolen Season

A Stolen Season: Bath

A Stolen Season: London

Scandalous London

A Gentleman's Promise

A Captain's Order

A Marriage Made in Mayfair

High Seas & High Stakes

His Lady Smuggler

Her Gentleman Pirate

A Wallflower's Christmas Wreath

Daughters Of The Gods

Banished

Guardian

Fallen

Stand Alone Books

Defiant Surrender

A Brazen Agreement

To Sin with Scandal

Outlaws

About the Author

Tamara is an Australian author who grew up in an old mining town in country South Australia, where her love of history was founded. So much so, she made her darling husband travel to the UK for their honeymoon, where she dragged him from one historical monument and castle to another.

A mother of three, her two little gentlemen in the making, a future lady (she hopes) keep her busy in the real world, but whenever she gets a moment's peace she loves to write romance novels in an array of genres, including regency, medieval and time travel.

Made in the USA
Las Vegas, NV
14 April 2024